DEDICATION

For Sheri deGrom,
the toughest, bravest and most beautiful woman I know.

And for Tom,
who was lucky enough to have her love.

ACKNOWLEDGMENTS

As always, my eternal gratitude to the amazing CJ Chase for her
late-night brainstorming, vigilant eye & razor pen.
(And, yes, I named my heroine after her.)

A huge thanks to my editor, Sue Davison, as well as Elaine
Eggert. I appreciate your eagle eyes & amazing feedback!

Finally, I owe a huge debt of gratitude to Ivan Zanchetta for his
gorgeous graphics & uncanny ability to pull everything together.

You're all incredible!

AIMPOINT

A US ARMY DETECTIVE REGAN CHASE NOVELLA:
BOOK 1 IN THE DECEPTION POINT SERIES

CANDACE IRVING

1

Your suspect is Special Forces.

Special Agent Regan Chase stared at the text on her cellphone, unable to move, unable to breathe, as the implications pummeled in.

Please, God. Let her be wrong. Perhaps her friend had jumped the gun.

Except, the text was from Mira Ellis. She never jumped. Not with her past. The woman was painfully cognizant of what could happen when a special agent piled incomplete evidence onto rumor and conjecture. Careers were ruined. Lives.

A follow-up text pinged Regan's phone, confirming her stateside colleague's usual zealous due diligence—and her own worst fears.

The warrant came through. See enclosed file. Off to see my boss. Will call soon.

Regan shot to her feet as she sent the file to her printer, rounding her desk to get a look at the papers already spitting out into the tray near the door of the tiny office deep inside the US Army's Criminal Investigation Division in Hohenfels, Germany. The door to the office opened as she retrieved the initial pages.

Yet another special agent—though this one was Army CID like her—entered, his laptop tucked beneath the right arm of his slightly wrinkled dark blue suit.

Agent Jelling tipped his thatch of strawberry curls toward the papers in her hand. "That the ballistics report we've been waitin' on?"

"Nope. Different case. These are phone records—from Mira." She collected the remaining pages from the tray as the printer wound down, glancing at the customer details on the uppermost sheet as she headed for the only other piece of furniture in her spartan office. The work table. "Her warrant came through; they belong to Scott Platt."

The Army—and Navy's—newest suspect of the hour.

Although Mira wasn't Army, she had a vested interest in the case since she'd initiated it when a sailor had walked into the Naval Criminal Investigative Service in Washington, DC, the day before. The sailor claimed he'd overheard a civilian he knew on the phone, discussing a pending terror attack in Germany. Mira had dug into the tip with a vengeance and discovered that not only had Scott Platt worked at the Pentagon, but he'd also been fired the previous summer. Mira had immediately brought him in for questioning. Platt was still refusing to talk.

Hence, the presence of the warrant and the records now in Regan's hands. "She thinks our guy's Special Forces."

Jelly's laptop thumped onto the table. "*Holy shit.*"

Regan nodded as she set the stack of papers down beside the computer. A thick yellow line bisected the uppermost page, highlighting a phone number corresponding to a call Platt had received the previous September, almost a year ago to the day. The call had lasted over an hour.

Mira had scrawled a name and rank inside the margin.

Jelly's freckled brow furrowed as he gave voice to both. "Sergeant First Class Evan LaCroix. Huh...I know that name."

"From where?"

"Not sure. Just know I'm familiar with it. And not in a good context."

"A run-in from the MP days?" They'd been friends since their first joint patrol as military policemen. She'd learned then that Jelly never forgot a name or a face. Getting promoted to Chief Warrant Officer Two alongside her four years ago and qualifying as an Army CID special agent had only enhanced his skill.

He'd just need time.

"Nah, that's not it. *Damn*." His hands came up to rub reddened eyes. "I'm raw today. The baby cried most of the night. Ava was so stressed, I took her midnight shift. It's left me chuggin' enough coffee this afternoon to satisfy even you."

"Yikes."

"It's a stage; it'll pass. As for that name, a photo might help." Jelly dragged his abused laptop around and opened it, quickly pushing through the requisite security protocols until he'd accessed the Army's personnel file on one Sergeant First Class Evan LaCroix, Special Forces.

The man's official uniformed photo greeted them, featuring cropped blond hair and an unnervingly baby-faced mug, along with the requisite green beret.

"Christ, he looks fifteen."

Regan checked the sergeant's birthday and did the math. Thirty-three. Definitely old enough to serve. And kill. But did this man possess the mindset to target his fellow soldiers—or worse, murder innocent civilians?

She waited as Jelly studied the photo at length.

Disappointment cut in as he finally shook his head. "I got nothin'." He glanced up. "Doesn't look like much of a terrorist though, does he?"

"They never do."

"True."

Regan studied the official photo as well, imprinting those baby blues and chipmunk cheeks firmly into memory. Jelly was right. Hardened Special Forces soldier or not, not only did that face not scream terrorist, it didn't even whisper big, bad snake eater. More like earthworm.

Then again, looks truly could be deceiving. She and the agent beside her had learned that the hard way, during the same knock-down, drag-out takedown in Iraq.

"You sure—"

"Wait! I remember him. Stateside. Three years ago. Fort Bragg." Disgust tinged Jelly's own bloodshot baby blues as he shook his head. "Man's a piece of *shit*."

"Then you did have a run-in with him."

"Nope. Never even met the guy. Ava did. We weren't married yet—had just met. Ava had recently transferred to Fort Bragg. So had LaCroix. He was the topic of conversation on post for damned near a month. Hell, a lot of posts. I'm surprised you never caught wind of it—oh, yeah. Right. You'd got called back to Afghanistan."

That explained it. But if Jelly didn't get to the point, she was going to throttle him, friend or not. "Damn it, what happened? What did he do?"

"Not what—who. LaCroix had a rep for hunting the young and newly commissioned. The younger and more newly commissioned they were, the more determined he was. Then, as soon as he'd bagged them, he'd dump 'em. He was quiet enough about it—at least outside of SF. But inside? They all knew. Anyway, three years ago, he focused on a nurse who worked the same shift as Ava. The nurse was so flattered the hound sniffing around was SF, she slept with him. Unfortunately, her commission wasn't the only thing she was risking. She was married with a kid. Her husband—some civilian doc Ava met a few times—found out and complained to the post commander. The nurse was so humiliated and terrified she was about to be court-martialed for an inappropriate relationship, she dropped the kid off with a friend for the night, went home and swallowed a bottle of pills. Her husband found her the following morning when he got off work. She'd been dead for hours. LaCroix didn't even bother to fake regrets to her folks when they came to collect her for the funeral."

"Jesus."

"Yeah." Jelly hooked a hand to the back of his neck and began to rub. "I'll bring up Bragg tonight with Ava, casually work my way around to the old gossip, see what else she knows about the guy."

Regan hid her wince. "You sure?"

Jelly might be a fantastic agent, but he was the lousiest of liars. Newborn baby or not, Ava could not be that sleep-deprived. No one could.

"Funny. *Fine.* I'll ask her while she's bathing the monster. She never looks away when she's doing that."

More like the former sergeant in Ava still knew when to keep her head down. Either way, Jelly's wife also knew how to keep her mouth firmly shut.

Probably why she and Ava got along so well.

Regan dropped her stare to the phone records. Their NCIS colleague had included the entire past year's worth.

Why?

She spread the papers out along the table, the knot in her gut tightening as she scanned line after highlighted line, noting dates, times and durations. Twenty-seven calls over the last year, almost evenly split between incoming and outgoing—and though most were ten to twenty minutes, at least five had breached the hour mark like that first call a year ago. Even more telling, every one of these longest five had been logged in the past six weeks, including the one their stateside sailor had overheard.

If LaCroix had been turned and if he was planning an attack, those recent, lengthening calls suggested an escalation. The hashing out of a plan.

Jelly leaned closer, squinting down at the records. "That's a hell of a lot of gab-time. Whatever he's planning, it's big."

Shit.

Regan stiffened. So did Jelly. They were both thinking it.

Again, it was Jelly who voiced it: *"Oktoberfest."*

Precisely. *Oktoberfest.* Their host country's infamous folk celebration of all things German was slated to begin roughly a hundred enticing kilometers southwest of Hohenfels...in fifteen days. Six million clueless, Bavarian-pretzel-savoring, beer-soaked revelers would be descending on Munich.

Six million targets.

They simultaneously shifted their attention to the photo on Jelly's laptop. To a blue-eyed, baby-faced blond who was more than capable of blending in long enough to execute whatever nefarious plot he contrived. Especially in Germany.

Jelly's whistle filled the office. "If your buddy's right about LaCroix—and my gut says she is—we're fucked."

She was about to agree when her phone pinged, alerting her to yet another text from DC, though this one had a slightly positive spin tacked on at the end.

Still in with boss—but on my way there. Flight details coming asap.

Regan texted back a thumbs-up emoji and slipped her phone into the pocket of her navy trousers. "I need to see Brooks. We need that phone tap and tail—yesterday."

Jelly shot her a grimace. "You know what he's gonna say, and how he's gonna say it."

She knew. But she wasn't asking. And she definitely wasn't

taking no for an answer again. She couldn't afford to. *They* couldn't afford to.

Regan swung around her desk to retrieve the suit jacket she'd left warming her chair's shoulders when she'd returned from lunch two hours earlier. She donned the jacket, shifting her dark, heavy braid over the collar and down her back as she headed to the table to gather up the pages of Scott Platt's records. "Keep reading that personnel file, will you? And take notes. I'll be back in a few to discuss them."

Hopefully, with her head still attached.

This time, Jelly laughed. Sort of. "Good luck, Prez. You always were braver than me. Must be that presidential juju you channel from your namesake."

Wrong. She wasn't brave—just stupid.

And desperate.

Platt's phone records in hand, Regan abandoned Jelly and headed out through the maze toward their boss' office. Like Mira, she could feel this one in her bones. Evan LaCroix was the real deal. If he had been turned, something was about to go down. Something big. Maybe Munich, maybe somewhere else.

Unfortunately, neither she nor Jelly had been able to convince their boss that the sailor's tip was sound, much less that Captain Brooks needed to pull out all the stops to support it. They both knew why. Hell, the whole blessed command knew, if not the entire US Army and most of their nightly-news-watching citizens back home.

Brooks had been burned.

Heck, they all had. But no one else was still cowering in the corner of his office two weeks on, licking his wounds and bitching about it.

Make that shouting.

Regan heard the captain's bellow while she was still a good twenty feet from his door. She had no idea who was on the other end of that one-side conversation, because it ended with the loud slamming down of a phone long before she'd reached the wooden portal. She knocked anyway.

"Enter!"

Her commanding officer was on his feet, his ebony scowl locked into place as he slapped his own sheaf of papers into his outbox. Regan drew the door shut behind her, patiently waiting for her CO to vent the remainder of his fury on the lid of his laptop before she stepped up to his desk.

"Good afternoon, sir. I just received a text from—"

"—Special Agent Ellis. I know. That was *her* boss on the phone, sticking his Navy-owned prick in where it doesn't belong. Why? I don't know. They've got their own goddamned pond, and it's a bloody big one. Man should mind his own business and concentrate on pissing in there. But since he's refused, I'll tell you the same thing I just told him. Mira Ellis can fly over here and advise, but that's it. She will *not* be working this case. Nor will she be requesting a tap on Sergeant LaCroix's phone or asking for the manpower to tail him." His scowl deepened. "*Nor will you.*"

"Sir, Agent Jelling says the sergeant—"

"I know all about LaCroix and his exploits. Yet another asshole who can't keep his dick to himself. Yeah, he likes them young and out of bounds. So what? The women were all senior to him. It was their job to maintain good order and discipline. Not his fault or mine if they were personally horny and professionally reckless. And, yeah, I know about the suicide. It stinks—but it doesn't prove squat, and you know it. Nor do those phone records you've got clutched in your hands. We need more."

"With a tap and a tail—" Christ, *either* one. "—we'll be in a position to get—"

"*No.*"

"Sir, you—"

"—said no, and I meant it. And if you even think about going over my head and bleating to your mentor on this one, I'll have your badge. You bring me evidence—hard evidence—and *then* I'll risk a tail." The man's dark brown glare was as filthy and blistering as his temper had been for the past two weeks.

Regan focused her attention on the wall beyond the closely cropped silver dusting his temples as she jerked her own temper into line. The captain's office was as spartan as hers. Unfortunately, their mutual lack of decorating skills was about all she and Brooks had in common.

Especially these last two weeks.

She got it. His confidence had taken a hit. And, yeah, with cause.

Not only had the subject of their previous investigation turned out to be a victim of sour grapes, the entire case had blown up in CID's face when the lieutenant they'd been investigating discovered he had a tail. To the entire command's misfortune, the lieutenant had taken the discovery to his uncle —a beleaguered US congressman. To deflect attention from issues with his constituency regarding his ongoing crappy behavior, the congressman had in turn raised indignant hell with the Pentagon, who in their turn had duly rained that same hell back down on the beleaguered military police captain still glowering at her from the opposite side of his desk.

Brooks had been lucky to escape the resulting shitstorm with his career intact. And from the fear still embedded in the whites of his eyes, the professional wounds were far too fresh for him to risk drawing the Pentagon's ire again—along with his own commanding officer's.

Nope. Brooks wasn't about to attach a tail to LaCroix. She wasn't even sure he'd risk it with direct evidence.

The hell with it.

Regan slapped the phone records on his blotter and shoved them across the desk until they were flush with the lid of his laptop. "Sir, I know the situation's dicey, but we don't have a choice. These records prove it. The calls between Platt and LaCroix have been lengthy and consistent—occurring every other Saturday or Sunday for the past year. The latest call matches the timing of the conversation that stateside sailor overheard last Saturday. Furthermore, six weekends ago, the frequency and duration of the calls tripled, and they haven't let up. If LaCroix has been turned, he appears primed to pop. *Oktoberfest* would be a truly devastating target, and it's still a full two weekends away. If we can get a tap into place—"

"You think he's not *ready* for that? Expecting it? *Dicey?* The man's a fucking Green Beret. If he's plotting something, he's taking precautions. And he sure as hell's checking to see if some bumbling carrot top in a suit's attached to his ass."

Christ. It wasn't Jelly's fault he'd been made.

Not only had the lieutenant been tipped to Jelly's physical description, the information had been passed on *while* Jelly was following him. She'd told Brooks that at the time. Shown him the irrefutable proof. Not that she'd risk their current need for a tail on LaCroix by dragging it all up again. Let alone reminding her CO that neither she *nor* Jelly had believed there'd been cause to follow the lieutenant in the first place.

Not with Brooks' mood.

She clamped down on her own foul temper once more and kept a firm grip on it. Once upon a time, she'd hoped the prior-enlisted status she and Brooks shared as combat-forged sergeants would allow them to find common ground as they worked to cull the occasional rotten apple from deep within the Army's core.

She'd been wrong.

As much as it would burn, it was time to drag out the knee

pads and commence the official begging. She didn't have a choice. "Sir, I know you're—"

"Save it, Chief. You don't know shit. Neither does Ellis. I neither want nor need that disgraced squid-cop here. All the two of you and that carrot sidekick have are hearsay and a bunch of calls. According to Agent Ellis' boss, Platt and LaCroix shared the same neighborhood in Shitsville, Alabama."

What? "Then—"

"No, that fact does not necessarily support you three. Those men could've been planning their fifteen-year high school reunion for all we know."

Except their source of *hearsay* had risked his career to report otherwise—and the sailor's timeline had been backed up.

Regan pushed forward, into the edge of the captain's desk. Into him. "That's why we need that tap. We need to know for certain. We can't afford to be gun-shy."

Wrong word to use.

Her boss' stare fairly smoldered as he leaned right back into her. "You got hearing damage from the firing range? I said, *no.* You want to make that a yes—go get me some goddamned probable cause. Something so juicy I can see, hear and taste it when I pass it up the chain. You said it yourself; you have two weeks. You're supposed to be some Second Coming savant when it comes to honeytraps. Not that I've seen it, mind you. I've had you squirreled away in that back office for eighteen months to shield your pretty face from the bulk of the soldiers who move through this post. And in all that time, you've done squat."

"Excuse me?"

"Yeah, I know. You've done your thing for the provosts at Baumholder and Wiesbaden."

And Grafenwoehr, Landstuhl, Stuttgart and Kaiserslautern— but who was counting? Evidently, not Brooks.

Nor was she thrilled with the way he was now eyeing her

naked face, basic braid, and minimally tailored suit. Especially when he offered up his first eager nod since he'd barked her through the door of his office. "Yup. I've changed my mind. Shit, I should've approved it yesterday. Well, I'm doing it now. Go slap on some lipstick and a tight skirt, and get that bastard's attention. You've put out for the rest of Germany; it's about time you put out for us."

The implication behind that double entendre was deliberate and ugly, and Brooks knew it. She ignored it. She knew full well he wasn't so much as pissed at her, as stinging from that gun-shy comment. Because he knew who it had been really directed toward. Just as he also knew that, deep down, it fit.

But she'd make him pay for it. In people.

"And Agent Jelling?"

"Take him. It's not like I want him touching anything else around here."

Go for broke. "And Special Agent Ellis?"

Yet another nod.

Hallelujah. It seemed miracles were still possible in her world.

"But Ellis is strictly emergency backup; that's all. I don't like that woman, and I don't trust her. The way you collect these lost souls baffles the hell out of me."

Oh, for Christ's sake. Mira had been exonerated years ago. Heck, it was why she'd turned her back on the Navy's *mea culpa* and its offer to reinstate her into its nuclear power program and joined NCIS instead. It was also why Mira understood Regan and her own motley collection of demons in a way no one else could.

She opened her mouth to defend her friend, but her boss spoke first.

"Doesn't matter. Ellis and her considerable baggage are not my problem, so long as you keep her away from me. According to her CO, Ellis will be here by zero six hundred, whether I approve or not. You might as well abuse her. The woman can do research on the fly with Jelling. Hell, she can even hold your virtual hand in the ladies room while you're out and about doing your thing to reel in LaCroix. But she does *not* go near him. Nor does Jelling. I don't want either of them fucking this up. Understood?"

She bit down on her tongue and nodded.

Brooks was still livid enough that he'd find a way to revoke Mira's assistance. No matter who'd approved it.

"Yes, sir."

"Then get to work, Chief. Give me what every other post's provost has been raving about on this side of the Atlantic. But be goddamned vigilant. Because if you're right and your performance is off, by even a fraction of a whiff, we'll have a nightmare on our hands. Not only will LaCroix be tipped off, but anyone else he may be working with will be in the wind, never to be seen again. At least not by us. So find an in with that asshole and get what we need, and do it soon. Before the bodies start piling up—in Munich or elsewhere."

Regan nodded crisply and scooped Platt's phone records off the desk, then turned around to exit the office. She was halfway to her own when her phone rang.

Mira's name flashed across the screen as she retrieved it. "Speak of the devil. I understand you'll be landing in time for breakfast tomorrow. Need a ride?"

"Yes. But there's another reason for my call—and it's not good."

Regan juggled the sheaf of papers in her hand as she elbowed her way through the door of her office. She didn't mind that Jelly was absent for his first official briefing since that fiasco. She had bigger worries.

Somehow, she knew what had happened.

LaCroix. "He called Platt's phone, didn't he?" The one NCIS and the DC Metro Police had confiscated when Scott Platt had been brought in and booked into a cell to keep his uncooperative mouth from doing a one-eighty and flapping open long enough to tip off his good buddy LaCroix.

"Ten minutes ago."

On a Friday? At fourteen hundred? They were six hours ahead of the East Coast, making it eight in the morning on Platt's end. Worse, it was a deviation from their Saturday/Sunday call pattern.

One that did not bode well.

Regan dumped the phone records on her work table and picked up the folded square of paper Jelly had addressed to her. "Did LaCroix swallow it?"

"I think so. Hell, I hope so. The Intensive Care Unit nurse we had manning Platt's phone was nervous, but I'm pretty sure she pulled it off. She threw in enough medical jargon to stump me. If we're lucky, her critical accident and coma story bought us some time. How much, we won't know unless LaCroix decides to call via the hospital's main line to confirm. If he does, the rest of the unit's nurses and physicians are prepared to back her up. But if some unsuspecting doc from another floor walks by and picks up that phone, the cover story could fall apart and fast."

The clock was ticking then, in more ways than one. "Understood."

"How's it going on your end?"

Regan sank into the metal chair at the table. "Not as well as I'd hoped, but it's getting there. Brooks shot down the tap and tail again, but he's regrown his pair enough to finally decide to send me in. I've got some research and planning to do, but I'll have my cover identity worked up before you arrive."

"I'll let you get to it, then. See you soon. Wish it was under better circumstances."

"Ditto."

Regan hung up the phone and opened the note Jelly had left.

Went home to grill Ava. Not even going to try to lie. We both know she won't say a word.

Back soon—J

Jelly's tactic was sound. But since Brooks wouldn't agree—especially with his current, added, ire toward her fellow agent—she took the time to walk the note over to her shredder. She fed the hungry beast and headed for her desk.

With the basics of her cover already churning through her brain, she phoned Public Affairs next.

Unfortunately, Terry Vaughn wasn't in.

She left a message for the stalwart captain who'd covered for her brilliantly on several missions before—albeit on posts other than Hohenfels and nearby Vilseck, including a war zone.

After hanging up her second call in twice as many minutes, Regan turned her attention to her laptop. She fired up the computer and clicked through the security protocols to access LaCroix's official Army record. She'd need to study his entire career history, as well as his performance evaluations, before she finalized her cover details with Terry anyway.

But this particular file would have to be absorbed quickly.

In light of the unusual timing of the sergeant's most recent stateside call to Platt's phone, the stakes had been raised even higher than those she'd just conveyed to Brooks.

Several pages into LaCroix's personnel record, they shot into the stratosphere.

Sergeant LaCroix wasn't just the real deal. He'd all but crafted it.

And it was born of C4, det cord and so much more. Before Special Forces had tapped LaCroix on his shoulder to invite him into the hallowed brotherhood, he'd been a sapper. But not just any sapper. LaCroix was so good at constructing both complex bombs and simple, impromptu explosives, he'd been tasked with teaching his fellow combat engineers at the Army's Sapper Leader Course at Fort Leonard Wood, Missouri.

Whatever his pending target might be, it appeared the man wouldn't even need a brick of C4 and handful of blasting caps to obliterate it.

Ice crackled along Regan's spine as she read one particular write up.

Sergeant LaCroix is an outstanding soldier and unsurpassed as a sapper. Though young, he possesses an uncanny and unparalleled ingenuity in crafting field-expedient explosives. I have the utmost faith in Sgt. LaCroix's ability to link up with any indigenous force to which he's assigned and quickly teach them to rig bombs with whatever's on hand. If the materials don't exist, Sgt. LaCroix will create them—and the results will be devastating.

The enemy will never see him coming.

The evaluation had been filed six years earlier. Since then, LaCroix had completed the SF Q Course and donned the vaunted green beret. As Special Forces, he'd gone on to serve four more tours in Afghanistan, Iraq and Syria, where he'd undoubtedly honed those innate, deadly skills of his to a terrifying proficiency.

And there was Hohenfels.

If LaCroix was up to no good, he had plenty of places right here in his own backyard to prepare for it. Far too many for CID to search.

Hosting the Joint Multinational Readiness Center, the forty thousand acre Army installation was the second largest combat maneuvering facility for US troops in Europe. Hohenfels' often unforgiving topography was riddled with thick forests and deep, often inaccessible ravines—wet and dry.

And that wasn't the worst of it.

With the JMRC training roughly twenty-two hundred

soldiers a day—sixty thousand last year alone—the installation's instructors and students chewed through a staggeringly large supply of munitions.

A staggering supply to which a trusted, outstanding sapper-turned Special Forces sergeant first class with an *uncanny and unparalleled ingenuity in crafting field-expedient explosives* would surely have been entrusted with near-unfettered access.

Brooks was right about one thing. Dicey didn't begin to cover this case.

She had to find a way to get close to LaCroix, and now. Because if they didn't have an entire team of savvy, adaptable agents trailing behind the man, twenty-four seven, ready to take him down *before* he managed to place that bomb, they'd never find it.

Not until it was too late.

2

Regan took a sip from her drink as she glanced at the mirror dominating the wall behind the counter of the off-post Bavarian bar. Between that oversized reflective surface and the etched-glass belly of a perfectly positioned grandfather clock across the room, she had a clear view of tonight's quarry: Sergeant First Class Evan LaCroix.

This was supposed to be the meet.

Their meet.

And yet, the sergeant was still glowering into his stein of beer, as he had been for most of the night. Despite her CO's backhanded phrasing, Brooks had been dead on about one thing. After three years as an MP and four more with CID, this was nowhere near her first time dangling from the proverbial hook. But it was the first time her target was more interested in his booze than in the bait.

Irritatingly, his friend wasn't.

From her vantage point, Regan caught the latest lingering assessment from LaCroix's behemoth of an escort. She ignored it, just as she'd ignored every other stare from the interloper since his arrival ten minutes earlier.

Instinct warned her she wouldn't be so lucky with the local off her right, doggedly edging closer until he'd reached the padded stool beside her. *"Kann ich Ihnen ein Getränk kaufen?"*

Regan infused her brow with wholesale confusion as she turned toward the twenty-something beanpole. "I'm sorry; I don't speak German."

Liar. She might not be fluent, but she'd picked up enough to know when she was turning down a drink.

Fortunately, the beanpole bought the brushoff and melted away.

Thank God.

Relief churned right back into frustration as Regan aimed another bouncing glance at the ornate grandfather and its reflective belly. She'd swear LaCroix was avoiding her. Worse, the colossus beside him was still sizing her up.

She was certain when the hulk leaned over to say something to the sergeant, then nodded—toward her.

LaCroix glanced up from his phone and stared at her for all of two seconds, before jackknifing to his feet.

Shit. Had she been made?

Scratch that. She relaxed. Her cover was intact.

That wasn't recognition biting into the sergeant's flushed features. Hell, LaCroix's attention wasn't even focused on her. He was glaring at his phone again. As his grip shifted, she could make out the dim glow of the screen as it flashed amid the clock's generous belly. A text bubble. One that had succeeded in extracting the only emotion she'd seen in the sergeant this entire Sunday evening—fury.

"Fuck!"

The hulk grabbed LaCroix's arm amid the sudden silence and pointed stares from the surrounding tables, clearly hoping to ease the sergeant back into his seat without creating more of a scene than he already had. LaCroix shook his friend off. Panic threaded through Regan as he swung away from the table. But instead of storming out of the bar, the sergeant stalked deeper within.

The pockets of German chatter and clinking of steins and glasses resumed as LaCroix turned into the hall that lead to the latrines.

Once again, her relief was short-lived. This time, as the only soldier whose interest she had succeeded in hooking tonight stood as well.

He was headed straight for her.

All too quickly, the behemoth had cut a path through the sporadically populated tables to stand beside her at the bar. Make that, tower over her. At six-three, easy, he rivaled the beanpole she'd shot down earlier, but with an added eighty pounds of muscle. Every ounce of which appeared to have been forged in the cauldron of combat too, judging by the trio of inch-long scars digging into the left edge of his darkly stubbled jaw, not to mention the thicker pair that tangled all the way down his neck to end somewhere beneath the collar of his black pullover. And that didn't account for the mottled rope feeding up his right forearm.

The arm currently heading her way with an equally large, scarred paw attached to its end. "Captain John Garrison, US Army Special Forces."

And that confirmed it.

She pushed a slight smile to her lips, not bothering to infuse it with sincerity, much less interest. "A soldier."

"Guilty as charged."

Agreed. But of what else? Plotting a terror attack?

Because his barhopping buddy was. The more she'd dug into LaCroix's life these past two days, the more certain she'd become. There was something off about the man, and it didn't have anything to do with who LaCroix preferred to screw.

Although she wasn't here to hook *this* man, the two had seemed awfully close at that table. And both were SF.

Was the captain in on it?

The unmet paw finally retracted. A moment later, its unfazed owner used that same paw to lift her leather shoulder bag from the seat beside her. He carefully settled the bag on the bar before commandeering the now empty stool with a finesse the beanpole would've envied, had he stuck around. Hell, it even impressed her.

Regrettably, the captain's interfering interest did not.

She had until LaCroix returned to get rid of him.

Unfortunately, he'd leaned closer. "So, you're American. Civilian? Or are you stationed at Hohenfels, too?"

She fielded the captain's curiosity with her own. "Special Forces? Am I supposed to be impressed?"

"Trust me, it's not all it's cracked up to be. At least not today."

An intriguing response, made more so by the shadows that momentarily flickered amid the depths of that steady stare. Both succeeded in ratcheting up her suspicions. And there was his name. Garrison. She'd come across it while prepping for tonight. John Garrison wasn't just Special Forces, he was LaCroix's former A-team leader. Not to mention, he and LaCroix resided in the same apartment complex.

"And your name is...?"

Regan fielded that question with silence.

"Ah, a woman of secrets."

He had no idea.

The captain met her noncommittal shrug with a nod—and raised her a slow smile. "I don't mind."

Odd. Most men did—especially the ones she ended up arresting. No matter how gigantic they were.

This one shrugged. "I'm a patient man. Persistent." The smile strengthened, causing a deep, dimpled fold to cut in on the right. "Motivated."

Perhaps. But, he wasn't as persistent as her. Definitely not as motivated. Without the glut of her so-called life lessons to draw upon, how could he be?

And there was the date on the calendar. The one relentlessly whittling down to *Oktoberfest*.

For the first time since he'd entered the bar, she studied the captain. This close, his hair appeared lighter than she'd first thought. More a medium brown. His jaw was too hewn and squared-off to be handsome, his brow and cheekbones too raw and prominent. He was arresting, all the same. No doubt because of that enormous frame. Those intimidating shoulders and bulging biceps. Hell, every inch of the man was intimidating, and she was not easily intimidated.

The scars didn't help. They made him appear harder. Aloof. In the end, it was that deep fold that saved him.

Until the man's innate arrogance kicked back in. "Well?"

Her name. Damn. He was persistent.

Where the devil was LaCroix?

For that matter, where was Mira? The woman should've put in an appearance by now. Though Brooks had remained firm on her friend's backup-*only* status, Regan wouldn't have thought anything could've kept her away. After an entire weekend holed up at CID along with Jelly, combing through every facet of LaCroix's life, Mira was as anxious as they were to get this operation going. To take the sergeant down.

Regan glanced at the door to the bar as it swung open, ushering in a group of rowdy locals with cheeks ruddy enough to suggest all were well past ordering their first round of the night. No NCIS agents in sight.

And still no sign of LaCroix.

Surely he'd managed to pee by now. Or was LaCroix on his

phone? Responding to that rage-inciting text? Plotting his end game.

And, damn it, did it involve six million innocent people?

Resigned to the wait—barely—Regan returned her attention to the steady stare that had been focused on her up close and from afar these past twenty minutes. If she stalled any longer, she risked converting the interest still brimming within into annoyance—and absence. While she certainly needed the latter, Garrison just might be insulted enough to drag LaCroix off with him.

If the sergeant ever bothered to return.

She held out a hand. Garrison's paw returned instantly, engulfing it. "Second Lieutenant Rachel Pace, US Army—Public Affairs. And, yes, I'm so green I checked into my first command three days ago." Because according to Ava Jelling's gossip, that was how the predatory SF sergeant liked them.

But while this SF soldier's whistle was low and teasing, it carried a surprising tinge of respect. "Three days? That is green." The captain's reluctance at losing her hand might have been charming, had he not motioned for the bartender to refill her drink—without even asking her. "Public Affairs. You're reporting to Terry, then?"

"Yes." As expected, he'd been more than willing to help out. She was now wondering if abusing their friendship for a case on Hohenfels was wise.

Terry. Not Terrance or Captain Vaughn, as most of the Army referred to the man.

She made a mental note to press Terry for information regarding his relationship with Garrison as the bartender stepped up to retrieve her nearly empty glass. He slotted a fresh one in its place and left.

Regan tipped her head toward the empty spot of polished walnut in front of the captain. "You're not drinking."

"Neither are you."

"It's club soda."

"I know."

He'd been studying her, yes. But that closely? She carefully gauged his former vantage point in the bar's mirror. Without the complementary reflection from the glass that the clock provided from this end, he couldn't have had a clear view.

So, how—

His smile dipped back in, underscoring a healthy hint of that dimpled fold. "I can smell the CO_2."

Ah.

The fold deepened as he leaned closer, invading her personal space. "So, you came to a bar for a...refreshing round of club soda?"

She shook her head. "I was supposed to be meeting a friend." A so-called friend she'd coldly murder in her sleep—or, at the very least, torture for a solid week—for not getting her ass here in time to deflect this guy.

The captain hadn't been kidding; he was persistent. Infuriatingly so.

Worse, he'd managed to shift closer. That enormous chest was now obscuring her view of the entire bar. A full, three thousand-strong brigade of NCIS agents could be marking time behind the man and she'd never know.

Regan took the ready excuse to lean precariously to her left, ostensibly to check the door for her MIA friend—as she scanned the hall leading to the latrines.

Still no LaCroix.

"And this friend...*she* still hasn't shown?"

Regan shook her head as she straightened. "No, *she* hasn't —yet."

"Excellent." He eased off, returning command of her personal space to her.

Definitely an alpha dog. One so sure of himself, he didn't feel the need to push it, or her, unless actively thwarted. So how the hell did she get rid of him? Because like a rottweiler with a meaty bone, this guy had no intention of letting go.

And then she saw it—him.

LaCroix. The sergeant had finally finished whatever he'd really been doing in the latrine, but the fury she'd noted at that incoming text hadn't cooled. If anything, it appeared to have been nurtured into an almost palpable rage.

Garrison had noted it too. "Excuse me. I need a minute."

"Of course." *Take a thousand.*

Intent on providing him the opportunity, Regan stood as well, adjusting her pink sweater over her faded jeans as she waited for the captain to return to his barhopping buddy. Once Garrison was seated—and speaking—she shouldered her leather bag and headed for the doorway from which LaCroix had returned.

Ears straining for the slightest clue, she caught Garrison's muttered, "*Damn it. I said I'd deal with it,*" as she passed their table.

Shit. Perhaps she'd attracted the right man after all.

Unwilling to risk blowing that attraction, Regan kept walking, turning down into the narrow hall, passing the men's latrine to reach the women's. It was possible she'd missed Mira's arrival, especially if her friend had entered the bar while that massive torso had been blocking her view of the door.

The main area was empty.

A quick dip and scan beneath all three wooden doors at the far end confirmed the stalls were vacant too. Where the hell was she?

Regan unzipped her bag, her fingers wedging up against her 9mm Sig Sauer's hidden compartment as she retrieved the phone she'd silenced before entering the bar.

No missed calls, no texts. Not that Mira would've risked either without a true emergency brewing. Her friend was safe.

Regan returned the phone to her bag as she headed for the sink. Given the Old-World Bavarian charm of the bar beyond, the angular spout was jarringly modern. The reflection in the mirror above, more so. Neither the green eyes staring back at her nor the blond, tousled "beach" waves tumbling down her back were hers. The temporary color and curl job was due to the skill of the stylist she'd visited the previous afternoon. The background file Agent Jelling had compiled suggested LaCroix's preference for both.

The tinted contacts had been her call. They helped her separate herself from the woman in the mirror, enhancing her ability to become Rachel Pace or...whoever.

They usually did.

They should. She'd been slipping in and out of the real Regan Chase since she was six years old. These past few years, she'd simply figured out how to draw on the talent for Uncle Sam's benefit. Every time she did—and succeeded in taking down a dirty soldier or a flat-out terrorist in the process—it helped to quiet the doubts within.

But would it ever be enough?

Regan braced herself as the bathroom door swung open—Garrison had been that determined—only to relax as she caught the smoother, born-blond strands of her friend. She rounded on her as the door closed. "Where the hell have you been?"

Mira stiffened, panic edging into eyes as blue as her own had been that morning. "What happened? Are you okay?"

Regan waved off her concern, embarrassed at the desperation she'd heard—in her own voice. "Sorry. It's been a long day." A longer evening. One that, in light of what she'd heard on the way in here, was about to get longer.

Mira blew out her breath. "No worries. I'd planned on getting here before you, but I got stopped on my way out of your office. I caught another case. Well, mission. Get this, since I'm still in Germany, and your boss has refused to let me do more than hold your purse, NCIS decided to loan me out. A security gig for some Turkish general. No details yet, so I don't know how much juggling will be involved."

Crap. She had details. Several big ones. Any of which could be significant. And now she'd lost her dedicated backup. "Great."

Mira's brow rose. "You said you were good to go."

"I am." Mostly. "It's nothing Jelly and I can't handle. Though I'm beginning to doubt Ava's gossip regarding LaCroix. He's just not biting—but his friend is."

"The gorilla at the table?"

"That's the one." Like her, Mira wasn't fond of muscle-bound men, and for the same reason. "He's—wait—they're both still out there, aren't they?"

Had she made a mistake in coming in here? Had she caused them to lose track of LaCroix?

Her panic eased as Mira nodded. "Yeah, they're there. Huddled up and hashing through something intensely by the looks of it. I couldn't make out what they were saying as I passed. Given their huddle and no sign of you, I was worried you'd slipped in here to send an SOS."

"No, I was just creating space. Trying to shake the big one. Name's Garrison. He's a captain. Also SF. I think I need to switch my aimpoint." *Think*, hell. She *knew*. She just hadn't wanted to accept defeat so easily. Especially since they could ill afford it.

Still, the strategy shift might not be a bad thing. Agent Jelling had focused on Garrison and LaCroix's records while she'd scripted and arranged the details of her cover. Everything in Jelly's brief had pointed to Garrison being in the clear.

But what if they'd missed something? Something that would explain that comment.

"As I said, LaCroix is *not* interested. Garrison is. Also, on my way in here, I heard Garrison say, *'Damn it. I said I'd deal with it.'*"

"You think they're both in on it?"

"Maybe." Regan channeled her frustration into a sigh. "I only had time for a cursory look at Garrison's file. Though Jelly cleared him, I figured I'd need the basics if I ran into him, since they live in the same complex. His file's squeaky clean. Though it did appear to be loaded down with a number of the Army's heaviest medals." Which meant the captain had also endured the barrage of back-to-back combat tours and drumming stress that usually went with earning those medals.

And there was that look in his eyes when they'd begun talking. It still gave her pause. Garrison could be burned out or just having one hell of a shitty week.

Like her.

And hers hadn't even gotten started yet. Not the worst of it.

Professionally or personally.

Regan pushed out another sigh. It didn't help any more than the previous one. "I don't have a decent enough bead on Garrison to gauge him."

Doubt pinched her friend's brows. "Platt didn't give me the impression there was a third asshole on this. Nor were there any calls to Garrison or any other SF colleagues."

True. But, "Platt may not have known." Nor did they. Not really. That was what was so maddening about this. Especially on her end. Unlike Mira, she hadn't even been able to question Scott Platt, much less get a bead on *him*.

As for LaCroix, a Navy SEAL Mira knew—who also knew LaCroix—had come through with a bit more information the night before. According to the SEAL, LaCroix's attitude had been on a downward spiral for the past year. The SEAL hadn't known why.

Would Garrison?

And did the captain share LaCroix's deteriorating attitude?

They needed to find out, and soon. As much as she hated to admit it, Brooks was right. That call their stateside sailor had overheard and those phone records were still circumstantial at best. The SEAL's opinion, hearsay. They needed hard evidence linking LaCroix to terrorism. It was up to her to get that evidence. And as things stood tonight, there was only one clear path to obtaining it.

Garrison.

"Rae?"

She shook her head. "Just thinking." Planning. Because the decision had already been made. Since the moment she'd heard that comment as she passed Garrison's and LaCroix's table. "I'm switching my focus."

"The gorilla?"

"Yeah. Do you have time to go to my office? Pull up everything we have on him. Go over it again and see if you can find a connection to Platt." LaCroix had one. Lack of calls or not, if Garrison was involved in whatever was going down, there was a chance he was connected to Platt too. She'd need to know what that connection was if she hoped to abuse it.

"Consider it done. And you?"

"I'm still leaving here with someone tonight." Just not the one she'd assumed. No matter. Like any soldier, she accepted her targets of opportunity when and where she found them. And then locked and loaded.

"Be careful. The big guys often come with bigger egos. And they do so like to have them stroked."

That was what she was counting on. Unfortunately for the tenacious captain, his swollen ego was all she planned stroking.

Regan nodded and left the latrine. Ten steps down the hall and a short turn into the still-crowded Bavarian bar, she knew she'd made the right call. LaCroix might've been seated when

Mira arrived, but he was gone now. Garrison, however, was waiting. Even better, he too had vacated his table—to station himself beside the main door, every muscle in that mountainous body letting her know he had no intention of missing her departure.

He caught sight of her and headed over. "You still waiting for your friend?"

Regan shook her head. "Just got a text. Something came up on her end, so we've rescheduled. It's getting late anyway. I need to call a cab."

"You're staying on post? At the Sunrise Lodge?"

She nodded. "I haven't decided if I want live in town yet."

"You should. You'll see more of the locals and get a better grasp of the language. But skip the cab. And don't worry about your tab; I settled it. I'm parked outside. I'll give you a lift." He turned to push the bar door open before she could argue.

"You don't mind?"

The proprietary hand already grazing the small of her back to gently nudge her along assured otherwise. "Not at all."

The hand shifted as they cleared the bar, securely engulfing hers as he led her across the modest, but well-lit lot as though she was a leashed puppy. Regan bit back her irritation as he brought them to a halt beside the passenger door of a silver Wrangler.

She glanced about. "What about your friend? I don't see him." Damn it, she couldn't even name LaCroix. Not until Garrison did.

"He's already gone."

"I hope everything's okay."

Garrison's nod was clipped, determined. "It will be."

"You sure you wouldn't rather go after him?"

That dark gray stare sharpened—on her.

Crap. Too much, too soon. "He seemed upset."

The gray softened. As did his nod. "Sergeant LaCroix got some bad news. He'll work it out."

"Sergeant? He's Special Forces, too?"

Another nod, and decidedly back to clipped. The stare had sharpened again, too. Narrowed. "If you prefer the man over me, say so. I'll back off. But you should know, Evan's not in a good place. He hasn't been for a while. I wouldn't want you to get hurt."

She waited for the captain to offer more, but he didn't.

That trio of scars at the left edge of his jaw were spinning a story all their own, though. And it was fascinating. From this angle and directly under the lot's relentless fluorescent light, she realized the scars were longer than she'd thought—roughly two inches each. They cut down into his neck where the ends of two of them furrowed in around his carotid, as though embracing it. And in the middle? A lovely, tattling pulse point.

One that had begun to flag.

The captain had a tell. Quietly or not, it was ratting him out. She may have only just met the man, but he was invested in her answer. Intimately.

Regan deliberately softened her gaze. "If I was interested in your friend, I wouldn't be standing here with *you*." She watched as relief entered the storm, calming it—and that pulse—before she pushed into the rest. "But I confess, I am worried about him. Your sergeant wasn't just upset tonight. He was livid. I caught his reaction before he left for the bathroom; the entire bar did. He was still furious when he returned. Is he...okay?"

To her surprise, Garrison shook his head. "Not really. Evan's hurting. He has been for a while. He was involved with someone. It was pretty serious."

Something in his tone had her asking, "Was? As in...she's dead?" If so, that was something Jelly and even Mira's SEAL hadn't been able to glean.

Yet another of the captain's stunted nods followed. But this one was softer, infused with a genuine compassion that nearly slipped past her defenses.

Rachel's—and Regan's.

Surprised, she shored up the latter's and pressed on. She had a terrorist to thwart. "I'm so sorry. What happened?"

"She was a nurse. Working with an NGO in Syria—in the north. She was killed by an artillery round last year, shortly after we were ordered to pull out so the Turks could do their thing. Evan's mindset's been on a bit of downward spiral since, and lately it's been getting worse. Just do me a favor and stay away from the guy, okay? At least for now."

Turks? Something began to niggle. Coincidence...or a connection?

Maybe this wasn't about *Oktoberfest* after all.

"Rachel?"

She felt the calloused pads of the captain's fingers on her cheek. The contact pulled her from her thoughts a split second before she instinctively jerked herself from him. That damned hand. The one that, once again, had touched her without her permission.

"You okay?"

She dragged a distracted frown into place. "Sorry. It's just... that's *awful*." And it was. But that didn't excuse the taking of more lives. Because her gut was now telling her that was exactly what LaCroix was plotting. Revenge. And if her other suspicion was correct, she might've figured out how—and it did *not* center on *Oktoberfest*. But if she was right, the fallout could be just as deadly.

"Yeah, it sucks." The remote clicked as Garrison unlocked his Wrangler.

She drew on her patience as he opened the passenger door for her, touching her yet again as he physically guided her into the seat. When one of those obscenely muscular arms reached across her torso to latch her belt for her, she nearly lost it.

Good Lord, was she *two?*

He hooked that same, scarred forearm along the roof of the Wrangler, catching her gaze, and pointedly holding it, as he straightened. "So—you'll stay away from the guy?"

"That should be easy enough."

He shrugged. "Maybe. Maybe not. Evan's living with me at the moment. You might run into him when you come to dinner tomorrow. I make a decent stir-fry."

Oh, the man could flash that dimple all he wanted, but it would not take the sting from his innate arrogance. What had happened to patience?

"I did mention I was motivated, right?"

Yeah, well, so was she. Because she'd definitely attracted the right man's attention. He and LaCroix didn't just reside in the same complex; they inhabited the same apartment. A geographical distinction which could prove critical given what she'd just learned about the sergeant. If LaCroix was in mourning, her chances of attracting the man's attention had been slim to none from the start.

Regan tamped down on her adrenaline and nodded calmly. "Okay."

The captain's brow arched. "Okay to which? Staying out of Evan's way?" The brow settled into place as his smile—and that ego—took over. "Or dinner?"

"Both."

"Outstanding." He finally backed out of her personal space and closed the SUV's door before heading around to the driver's side to climb in and start the engine.

She was working through possible conversational threads for the coming drive when his phone pinged.

"Excuse me." He leaned forward to retrieve his phone from his back pocket, frowning as he focused on the screen.

"Is everything okay?"

"Hmm? Sorry." He clicked out of the screen and turned to her before she could get a look at whatever had caused that stare of his to blacken. "It's work. I need to head in. I'll drop you off at the Lodge and call you tomorrow with the details for dinner. What's your number?"

He tapped her digits into his phone as she rattled them off, then appeared to add something else before he switched off his phone and slotted it into the storage well behind the Wrangler's gear stick. Her phone pinged before they cleared the lot.

this is John

looking forward to tomorrow—and you

Ditto on her end. But for an entirely different reason. One she was continuing to hash through in the privacy of her own thoughts as he steered the Wrangler toward Hohenfels. Whatever had come up at his work had caused the captain to be as preoccupied as she was, because he didn't say a word during the drive.

He seemed surprised when they reached the Lodge without speaking.

"Thanks. I appreciate the lift." Regan grabbed the handle to the passenger door and opened it before he could climb out and do that for her too.

She wasn't quick enough. His right hand found her left before she could clear the seat. He squeezed her fingers. "Hey, sorry if I was distracted. It's just—"

"—your head's already in the game."

"Yeah." That dimpled fold made a brief appearance. Sheepish suited the man—and her—a lot more than arrogance. "So...I'll see you tomorrow?" As did actually asking.

"Yes."

The moment he released her hand, Regan bailed out and closed the door.

Garrison wasn't the only one headed to work. So was she.

Hopefully, Mira was already there, because they had some serious digging to do into an NGO's death from the previous year.

If her suspicions panned out, she'd not only zeroed in on LaCroix's motive, she'd identified the sergeant's true target. If so, six million visitors to *Oktoberfest* would be safe after all—at least from LaCroix.

But the current, precarious configuration of NATO was *not*.

3

Regan made it to CID within minutes. She parked her Explorer and pushed through the main doors, heading straight for her office. To her relief, Mira was already inside, absorbed in a file on the laptop she'd brought from the States.

The adrenaline still coursing through Regan's veins caused her to close the door behind her with more force than she'd intended.

Mira looked up. "Well, that was quick. Bad kisser?"

"Funny." She stepped up to her desk and hooked her hip onto the corner beside her friend's laptop. "What's the name of that Turkish general you're about to babysit?"

The smirk evaporated. Suspicion rooted into its place. "Why?"

"Because I think we have a motive—and a target. And it's not *Oktoberfest.*"

"Holy crap. That *was* quick. How the hell did you discover that?"

Regan crossed her arms. "The name? And his branch too,

please." She'd need that and a bit more before she'd risk saying the rest out loud—and jinxing it.

Mira knew it too, because she cursed beneath her breath as she dutifully swung her attention to the screen to click out of the file she'd been reading before opening another. "Principle's name: Aytaç Ertonç. General, Turkish Army."

"Infantry? Armor? Artillery?"

Please say Artillery.

"Hang on...." Mira scrolled down into the document. "Hmm. Don't see his branch. It might not even say." But she kept scrolling and scanning. "Aren't most Infantry, anyway? Or—wait; here it is." She glanced up, beaming. "Artillery."

"*Yes.*"

"And, why are we so excited by Artillery?"

Regan shook her head. Definitely not willing to jinx it. Not with six million lives potentially on the line. "I need coffee. While I'm gone, do me a favor? Pull up what we've got on known victims of Turkish Army artillery fire following our pullout of Syria last year. Specifically, female NGO medical personnel. I promise to reward you when I return." Meanwhile, she needed to get the taste of club soda out of her mouth and a ready hit of caffeine in.

"Fine—but pour two cups."

"You got it."

Mira was already minimizing the general's file as Regan turned to leave. She made a beeline for CID's coffee station and poured out the requisite cups, pausing just long enough to pollute Mira's with cream and sugar before she headed back.

The NCIS agent's Cheshire cat grin was setting in as Regan reentered her office to slide the contaminated coffee over. "What'd you find?"

"Five victims so far. Need names?"

"No." Garrison hadn't provided one. "Any of them between the ages of twenty and, say...forty?"

"Sure. Here's the first." She slid the laptop around so Regan could see the report. It contained a photo of a pretty black woman...but she'd been a doctor, not a nurse.

"Nope. Next."

Mira leaned closer and clicked the tab at the top of the screen. As she scrolled down the page, another photo popped into view.

They stiffened in unison.

"*Damn*. She's looks just like you, Rae. Well, how you look tonight."

"Yeah." Hand one to Ava Jelling. Her gossip regarding LaCroix's rutting preferences was spot on. Nor was Mira exaggerating. With her hair lightened and the tinted contacts she'd chosen, she and the woman on the screen could've been sisters. At the very least, cousins.

Regan scanned the photo's caption. "Carys Kaide. Scottish." *Nurse.* "She died as a result of Turkish artillery fire while they were pounding out Operation Peace Spring to create their 'safe' zone."

Irony didn't even begin to cover that one, did it?

"Hang on—" Mira swung the laptop her way and switched files. "I saw something while I was skimming...Yup, right here. General Ertonç—then *Colonel* Ertonç—headed up that Syrian bombing campaign. In fact—"

"—he made general off it." *Off Carys Kaide's death.* "Sorry. I know you hate when I finish your sentences."

"No. I only hate it 'cause you're always right. And, yes, Ertonç's career got a critical bump because of his actions in the same campaign that killed Carys. But I bet you didn't see this one coming..." Mira swung the screen out again. "According to this tidbit—and the call I took earlier in this office—the Ertonç security detail was originally scheduled to muster up a good five weeks from now, which is why I was co-opted. A number of the intended assets are still on other assignments. But the general arrived *tonight*—out of the blue and on his own dime. Not his government's, and not ours. Why? And why show so early? Even your boss doesn't have an explanation."

She didn't have an explanation either. Yet. But she'd stake her badge on the fact that LaCroix had been tipped off about the change in plans. "According to Captain Garrison, LaCroix and the nurse were serious. That mood deterioration your SEAL noticed? Garrison pinged on it too. It began with Carys Kaide's death. That text LaCroix blew up over tonight? It came in right around the time you were here, getting your orders to report for the Ertonç detail. Someone must've let the sergeant know his nemesis had arrived early."

LaCroix had been livid because the bastard who'd murdered the woman he loved was not only alive and thriving—but now less than ten miles away.

"You're right." Mira nodded. "Motive and target; we've got 'em both. I knew I was smart to bring this to you."

Yeah, well. Motive and target were all they had. And both were as circumstantial as the rest. Nor had LaCroix actually done anything wrong—that they could prove. If they brought him in for questioning and he clammed up like Platt, they'd lose any chance of figuring this out before it was too late.

And if Garrison was involved?

Damn it. She hated it when Brooks was right.

Regan purged her excess frustration with a sigh. "It's not enough." But she knew when and where she had a shot at gaining access to more. "I'm having dinner with the captain tomorrow at his place—and, apparently, it's LaCroix's too. I'm not sure when the sergeant moved in, but it seems he and Garrison aren't just friends. They're housemates." All the better for their investigation. Because if there was a way to finagle a look inside the sergeant's room and his private life, she'd find it. "I need to take another look at Garrison's file, LaCroix's too. Where's Jelly?" She hadn't spotted her colleague's freckled face and unruly strawberry mop on the way in.

"His wife called. Their two-month old spiked a fever. He left to meet them at the ER. Should I pull him back?"

"No. He'll have left me a printout of his notes in his drawer. I'll find them before I leave."

Dinner. Garrison. Reality bit in.

Hard.

Damn it, it was just a meal. She'd get in and out, unscathed. She had before. Many times.

She caught Mira's sigh. "Okay, spill it."

"Spill what?"

"Whatever's bugging you. You've got that look; you've had it since you marched in here."

She had a look?

Crap. She must. Because something was bugging her. *He* was bugging her. And not in a good way. Garrison hadn't noticed, had he?

"Well?"

"He's...handsy."

"*Jesus.* He didn't—"

"No." She'd have halted that instantly—and painfully. On his end. "The guy's just—" How could she put this? "He keeps touching me. It's..."

"Irritating?"

"Suffocating." All those...little touches. They made her feel trapped. As though she was a kid again with no say over her own body. No right to her own private space. Hell, no one made it through as many foster homes as she had without confronting it.

Though she'd been lucky. Because there was touching and

there was *touching*. And foster kids—girls, though yeah, some boys too—often got the twisted and very ugly end of the latter.

Regardless, this was going to be a rough one. Made rougher by an anniversary she'd been trying to ignore all week. Hell, all month. Unsuccessfully.

"You want to talk about it?"

"I'm fine."

"Bullshit. I'm sitting right here. I can see your face. And I can read a calendar. Tomorrow's bound to be a lousy day."

"I said, I'm good." To prove it, she stood. Or maybe it was just to escape that stifling sympathy. It was almost as claustrophobic as the captain's grabby grip. "I need to get those notes from Jelling's desk. Need a refill?"

Mira recognized the feigned urgency for what it was, but she shook her head—and let it go.

Regan took advantage of the reprieve before her friend could change her mind, departing to track down her fellow CID agent's notes. She found them right where Jelly usually left them. She retrieved the ever-thickening folder, which had her real name scrawled on a yellow sticky attached to the front, and returned to her office.

By the time she arrived, Mira's attention was fused to her glowing screen. *Thank God.* Regan had enough to deal with without churning up the rest.

She sank into the armchair beside her desk and hooked the heels of her leather boots over the edge as she cracked open Jelly's notes.

Two paragraphs in, it hit her. "Why are you here?"

Mira glanced up from her screen. "Uh, I believe you asked me to come."

"I mean still. Don't you have a security briefing to attend?"

"Nope." She tapped the top of the laptop's screen. "Got it all right here; it's a plug and play. I'm reviewing it now. Basically, I'm just precautionary backup to the backup, at least for tomorrow. My duties'll be reassessed after. No doubt once the Protective Service Unit's had a chance to see who they can grab to work the remainder of the job."

Regan closed the folder and dumped it on the corner of her desk. "Are you saying PSU's opening security posture is canned?"

Mira nodded. "At least the first gig. I'm to show up at an auditorium across post tomorrow at fourteen hundred for a kickoff speech by the general, followed by some special, invite-only meet-and-greet with the..." She glanced at her screen. "Wolverines."

Regan thumped her boots to the floor. "*Wolverines?* As in Special Forces? As in the training team to which LaCroix and Garrison *are currently attached?*"

Both men would be there. At that speech and most likely at the private meet-and-greet.

Worse, if PSU was using a canned protection scenario, there was an outstanding chance that same scenario was one LaCroix and/or Garrison had red-teamed and vetted—personally. In other words, they'd already know every possible weakness—and how to exploit it. Because they'd already done so.

"Shit."

Regan nodded. "Yup." The hell with waiting for tomorrow. The time to reassess her NCIS colleague's role was now. "I'll call Captain Brooks and clear it with him, but I want you on that detail twenty-four seven, starting tonight. Get as close as you can to Ertonç and stay there. At least until we're certain he's not the target."

And if her gut was right, and he was?

Hell, even if LaCroix hadn't vetted the security procedures they'd be using, Mira and that team had their work cut out for them. From the look in her friend's eyes, Mira knew it, too.

Along with the rest. The sergeant's attitude might've taken a downturn lately, but his skills had not. If LaCroix wanted Ertonç dead, there was an excellent chance the general would be six feet under, and soon.

And the fallout?

Turkey's relationship with NATO—and especially the US— had been hanging by a thread for some time now. Discovering that an American soldier had coldly assassinated their newest war hero-turned-general just might snap it.

Permanently.

MIRA ELLIS WAS MISSING in action—again.

Regan scanned the ocean of US Army and multinational camouflage as she neared the array of double-doored entrances to the auditorium. So far, there was nary a sign of her NCIS colleague.

Wait. *There*. Beside the doors to her right.

Regan focused on her friend's sleek blond updo and navy-blue suit as she slipped between a pair of British officers. "Pardon me. Just passing through."

She spared a smile for the shorter lieutenant's stumbling apology and kept advancing, repeating her excuse thrice more as she breached camouflaged cluster after cluster. Finally, she was firmly entrenched within the line leading up to the entrance doors beside which Mira was dutifully stationed.

The thickly lashed dart of blue sent her way assured Regan that Mira had spotted her as well, despite her own neatly secured French braid and Army Camouflaged Uniform with the corresponding second lieutenant insignia she'd donned that morning. But there'd been something else in that dart of blue, too. Her colleague had something to relay.

Something big.

Regan produced Rachel Pace's freshly minted ID as she reached the doors.

Mira glanced at the ID and motioned her through, leaning in to murmur in her right ear as she passed. "Your date's a CPF—and E's US man Friday."

Garrison? A Close Personal Friend? Of the general?

Regan forced herself to focus on the set of ACU-clad shoulders less than a foot from her face, following the camouflaged fabric into the rapidly filling auditorium as she processed her shock. She'd assumed the captain would be here this morning, yes, but as a faceless uniform among many. After all, he'd received his own text last night. The one that had him forgoing whatever moves he'd been intending to attempt with her and heading back to his office. That text had to have concerned the general's early arrival and the speech she was about to hear, along with the Wolverine meet-and-greet to follow. But Garrison was intimately acquainted with the general?

How intimately?

More importantly, was that cozy relationship behind the rest of Mira's man Friday message? Namely, Garrison's apparent selection as the general's Hohenfels US Army liaison. Or was there another darker, possibly more nefarious, reason?

Christ. She was getting whiplash.

By the time she'd finished studying the captain's file last night, she'd come to the conclusion that those shadows she'd spotted in his eyes at the bar had been born of nothing more than constant stress and lingering exhaustion. There was nothing in the captain's recorded past to suggest that, like LaCroix, he too had suffered a debilitating sucker punch to his innate sense of duty, honor and country. Let alone a concrete connection between John Garrison and Scott Platt.

"Damn it, I said I'd deal with it."

By the time she'd finished plowing through the captain's stellar performance evaluations and award write-ups, she'd convinced herself the comment referred to anything from a normal, work-related dispute down to and including quieting the volume on the TV at night.

Was she wrong? Had she missed something? Something that wasn't hinted at in the file, or simply hadn't yet had time to appear?

Had Garrison lobbied for the collateral duty because of his own souring take on the US Army in general and the SF mission in particular?

He had been in that bar with LaCroix. The US/Syrian-Kurd reversal in support and subsequent pullout had rattled a lot of SF cages. Did those shadows she'd seen point not to stress, but a growing, fundamental burnout?

She could've sworn he'd been talking LaCroix down following that explosion-inducing text. What if he hadn't been? What if Garrison been urging patience?

Her gut still leaned no. But what if her gut was off?

Could she afford to take the chance?

The answer—an absolute no—had Regan altering her path. Instead of taking a seat near the front of the auditorium, she opted for a spot near the center of the rapidly coalescing mass of bodies. She slipped in behind a pair of broad, beefy shoulders and immediately spotted two of her three current targets: a crisply ACU-clad John Garrison and this morning's surprisingly not quite larger than life guest of honor—a stocky, silver-haired, thickly mustached and somewhat wan-looking General Aytaç Ertonç. The men were marking time mid-stage right, near a trio of senior male US Army officers. Even from forty feet away, it was clear Mira was correct. Garrison and the general weren't simply friendly; the men were practically bosom buddies.

When had that happened? Where?

Why?

The answers would explain a lot. Potentially even exculpate the captain once and for all—or condemn him.

As she studied the curiously covert body language between the men, Regan compared and contrasted the facts she'd spent half the night gleaning. Though an officer now, Garrison had six years' time in service on his contemporary captains—because he'd begun his career as an enlisted combat engineer. Like LaCroix, Garrison had been the go-to expert at rigging explosives at his first command, and an even better leader. So much so, Garrison had been tapped for Officer Candidate School, then Special Forces.

All told, Garrison had served in a number of hot spot around the globe, but it was his first tour as an SF officer in Afghanistan that had most likely brought him into Ertonç's orbit. From what she'd also read in the general's intel file, both Garrison and then-Colonel Ertonç had been operating in and around Kabul at the time.

Doing what, she would love to know.

Whatever they'd done had forged a seriously tight relationship between the men, especially on Ertonç's side. How else to explain the general's noticeable reluctance as Garrison extricated himself from their conversation? Stranger still, the final nod Ertonç offered Garrison had an odd, almost deferential dip to it.

From a general to a captain?

Her curiosity rose as Garrison headed for the podium at the front of the stage to test the microphone. Her body, however, lowered as she instinctively used the beefy shoulders of the soldier in front of her for added cover and concealment while she studied the captain's features. The overt assurance and easy confidence she'd noted in the bar and parking lot last night were muted as the man ran through the sound checks. Because he was on a stage in front of several hundred soldiers?

Or had that intriguing conversation with the general affected him too?

The admittedly all too brief moments she'd spent in Garrison's company had Regan leaning toward the latter. Until the captain stiffened. Stared. The man was instantly and unequivocally livid.

With her?

Simply because he'd spotted her here?

Lord, she hoped not. Though he was twenty feet away, she'd definitely felt that spike of ire. If it was directed at her, she'd not only lost a dinner invite, there was no way Garrison would let her near his apartment, much less LaCroix's portion of it.

No. In the tense, motionless moments that followed, she became certain that cold stare wasn't focused on her, but someone just off her right. A row or two behind her.

Who?

Dare she risk turning far enough around to find out?

Regan forced herself to wait. To watch.

To study.

Garrison's outward demeanor calmed more quickly than she'd have thought possible as the man absorbed the brunt of his anger. It was still there, though. Seething, just beneath the surface. But a second later, it was gone. Another, and the captain had turned to cede the podium to an approaching US Army colonel.

"Good afternoon, Soldiers."

As the colonel launched into his introduction and brief overview of General Ertonç's career with the Turkish Land Forces, Regan finally risked turning her head, then her torso, just far enough to the right to identify—

LaCroix?

It was him all right. The sergeant was precisely where she'd anticipated. But not—from that look on the captain's face earlier —where Garrison had assumed the sergeant would be. Even more fascinating were the vestiges of fury she could see in LaCroix's still-hardened features. The sergeant was equally livid...with Garrison.

Why?

Fortunately, LaCroix was so consumed with his anger, he didn't appear to be paying attention to the crowd around him, including her.

She was invisible to him. For now.

Intent on remaining so, Regan carefully eased her torso toward the stage, hoping to catch another glimpse of the captain's expression, but she was too late. All she caught was the blur of those intimidating shoulders as they disappeared though the curtains at stage right. Moments later, she was joining the audience as they all stood, clapping to welcome General Ertonç to the podium.

The mass movement allowed her to catch to Mira's eye and receive a subtle nod in return. Mira had caught the fiery exchange between the captain and sergeant as well, and was just as intrigued.

Fortunately, her NCIS colleague was able to remain on her feet as Regan and the audience resumed their seats. By the time Ertonç had begun his opening remarks, Special Agent Ellis had shifted her position, smoothly posting herself just past LaCroix's row where she began to quietly mark time.

Just in case.

Regan forced herself to lean back. To relax and listen.

The longer she accomplished the latter, the more bemused she became. Aytaç Ertonç had an excellent command of English. So why was he using it to deliver a speech that was so bafflingly generic?

As the minutes passed, Regan couldn't help shifting in her seat, along with half the general's custom-made audience.

Like most everyone there, she'd suffered though countless mandatory doozies in her career. She also recognized a canned number when she heard it.

But this one? Other than a scant reference or two regarding the need for NATO armies to work together, there was just... nothing. No substance. Certainly, no detail. The general hadn't even tried to tailor his speech to this crowd.

What was Ertonç really doing in Hohenfels?

Because this was *not* it.

Before Regan knew it—before they all knew it—everyone in the audience was jackknifing back up to the soles of their boots, clapping respectfully as the general nodded once, then turned to depart the stage.

Just like that, the event was over.

Unfortunately, Terry Vaughn hadn't been able to secure her an invite to the one that followed. The meet-and-greet.

She had half a mind to risk Terry's ire, and possibly Garrison's, by crashing it anyway, when she noticed that LaCroix didn't appear to be on the select list of invitees headed toward the front of the stage either, because he was leaving. She turned to follow the sergeant out of the auditorium. If she could catch up with him, "accidentally" bump into him, she just might be able to—

Damn.

He'd disappeared into the drifting and shifting cloud of camouflage.

Where had he—

Yes. Regan caught sight of the sergeant's stiff spine and icy stride as she cleared the double doors she'd used to gain entrance to the auditorium not more than fifteen minutes earlier. Ten more steps and she'd be coming up alongside him as he departed the lobby.

Halfway into her impromptu quest, a hand locked around her right elbow, tugging her to a swift and sudden stop.

She spun around to confront its owner, only to snap her mouth shut as she spotted the same dark gray stare she'd spent a good deal of the previous night avoiding in that Bavarian bar. Garrison.

Shit.

While the ire she'd noted during that stage exchange had faded, rampant suspicion had burrowed into its place. And it was definitely directed at her.

"How the devil did you get in here?"

"Pardon?"

"The auditorium. That briefing you just attended was closed. *How* did you get in?"

Sorry, Terry. She'd taken the time to call him over lunch and warn him it might come to this. Terry had been decidedly unhappy with this particular backup plan, especially since it seemed he and Garrison were friends. But mostly because Terry knew he'd have to take the crap that was bound to come with what she was about to do.

Too bad. There was no way she was giving up Mira.

Regan slid a light, easy smile to her lips. "My boss."

"Terry?"

She nodded. "Captain Vaughn called me into his office this morning. He said there was a general who'd be speaking here this afternoon, then afterward with just the SF crowd—and that I should show up and do everything I could to score an interview with the man of the hour."

"General Ertonç?"

She shook her head as she kicked her smile up a notch, deliberately brightening it. "You."

4

Regan winced as that oversized grip shifted, clamping around her upper arm as its owner turned to draw her resolutely across the lobby toward a smaller, narrow doorway that went...somewhere.

Her irritation at once again being led against her will was supplanted by frustration as she caught sight of LaCroix's profile moments before Garrison nudged her into a seriously cramped, audio-visual storage closet.

Just like that, LaCroix was gone.

With him, any chance she'd had of subtly questioning him regarding that terse stare down he'd shared with the man now staring *her* down.

Garrison reached behind him to snap the door shut, shrinking an already tiny space exponentially.

"Explain." Hard. Clipped. Definitely an order. And not from the off-duty man in that bar last night, doing his damnedest to draw her out and engage her personal interest, but from the stiff, Special Forces captain looming two feet away.

Waiting.

Worse, that revealing pulse she'd noted beneath the fluorescent parking lot light was throbbing. This was not good.

She considered slipping on yet another breezy smile, then instinctively changed her tactics. To impatience. "I told you. My boss called me into his—"

The sharp shake of his head cut her off. "Not that part. Me. Why the hell would you want to interview me? And why now?"

So that was what was bothering him. Even more than her presence at an event which, as he'd stated, had been closed.

Of course, that revelation had her plotting to push it—and him—with half-truth, half-conjecture, and an entirely fervent prayer that this latest meeting of theirs wasn't about to blow up in her face before it got started. She crossed her arms, if only to keep any stray nerves from betraying her as that icy stare grew icier with every second that ticked by. "Why not you? You're the general's US liaison for the next few days. Who wouldn't be interested in reading about that? I also understand you two know each other personally, that you met years ago in Kabul. You're bound to have a unique insight into the man."

It was her turn to wait—for confirmation of what she'd just said. Any part of what she'd just said. She waited in vain.

"Who's your source?"

"I beg your pardon?"

"Your source. *Who* told you General Ertonç and I are friends?"

"You aren't?"

He ignored the question. "Who?"

Great. Once again, she was going to have to sacrifice Terry to that growing subzero vortex. If he survived the ensuing frostbite, he just might forgive her. Unfortunately, she had no choice. There was no source protection in her faux line of work. For a civilian reporter, yes. Not a military one. Not with the ever-present national security card at the top of Garrison's deck. Not if the public affairs officer in question wanted to keep his or her job—which she definitely needed to appear to want to do.

Or perhaps not. The camouflaged pattern on the captain's ACUs had given her another idea. Possibly, an out.

"I don't know."

"You—" He broke off. Frowned. "What?"

She shrugged. At least her answer had surprised him out of his anger. Best to capitalize on it quickly. "All Captain Vaughn knew was that you'd worked with the general in Kabul." And if Terry didn't, he was about to discover it and soon. From her. "I overheard the part about your friendship from a conversation between two soldiers seated near me during the general's speech. In fact, that's who I was following when you grabbed me and hauled me in here, or rather, who I was trying to follow. I was hoping to verify the information for my story, and perhaps find out more about your friendship with the general and how you two met, before I approached you about it."

There. Hopefully, the gabbing soldiers bit would assuage any lingering suspicion should he have spotted LaCroix's retreating form as well.

She waited several beats. When the captain didn't respond, she drew on her feigned irritation from earlier. "Well? *Are* you two friends?"

The nod he finally offered was curt. "Of a sort."

Well, that suggested...what?

This time, she did draw on that breezy smile. "Fantastic. Then perhaps you can assist me in getting the interview I'd really love to land?"

"Let me guess—Ertonç?"

She ignored the budding sarcasm in his tone as she deliberately infused hers with an eagerness that would've put the entire White House press corps to shame. "Yes. Captain Vaughn put in a request for one this morning, but he was shot down...by you? At least, I'm assuming so. From the interaction I saw up on the stage, it certainly looks as though you've been tapped as point man for the general's visit."

His thin smile offered a "nice try." But the slight uptick in that lovely, tattling pulse confirmed it. He *was* Ertonç's US man Friday.

But how did that intriguing collateral duty mesh with what she'd seen and heard in the bar last night between this man and Sergeant LaCroix? Not to mention the blistering stare down she'd just witnessed?

Suddenly, every instinct in her body converged—and she knew. She'd been collecting up the evidence in that revealing pulse and in the captain's body language, right here and right now with her, and earlier up on that stage with the general. Whatever LaCroix was plotting, Garrison was not in on it.

In fact, every tense, overly generous shred of sinew in his body underscored the opposite.

Garrison was trying to *protect* the general.

But from what? The captain wasn't privy to LaCroix's plans, whatever they were, or he'd have come in to CID and reported him. Garrison did know something, however, something about Ertonç. And he was actively working to conceal it from her.

But why? He had no idea she was a CID agent. That left her supposed job with Public Affairs. Which meant Garrison didn't want—couldn't afford—to have a reporter snooping around.

What had he said? "*Why the hell would you want to interview me? And why now?*"

Her interest in him wasn't the critical element so much as her timing. Last night he'd sought her attention with a tenacity she hadn't been able to shake, not without pissing him off and risking her case. The only thing that had happened between then and now was Ertonç's early arrival. She'd bet her badge that whatever Garrison was concealing from her had everything to do with the real reason Ertonç was in Hohenfels. The curious body language between the men on that stage and the perplexing deferential nod she'd observed confirmed it.

And so much more.

Garrison didn't need his new collateral duty to get close to Ertonç; he was already there. It was *Ertonç* who needed *Garrison*.

Regan tucked the stunning turnabout away and located the twin of the easy smile she'd begun all this with. She infused it with as much warmth and teasing as she dared as she leaned into the captain. "I should warn you: I'm tenacious. I already know that General Ertonç wasn't scheduled to give that painfully bland speech I just heard for another five weeks, and that his premature arrival has had everyone scrambling. So, why's he really here? Of course, I'm happy to take my curiosity, and go off and satisfy it myself. Or..."

She left the word dangling, exploiting the cloistered intimacy of the tiny closet he'd trapped them within to keep a host of other, more enticing, possibilities dangling as well.

Fortunately, she saw his hand coming up. She was able to brace herself as those callused fingers slid in to lightly cup her neck. His thumb scraped beneath her chin so he could tilt her face further up as he leaned down.

"...Or what?"

"Or you can help me get there first. *On* the record. And—" She allowed her smile to deepen, adding a hint of laughter as she stretched all the way up to his waiting ear to whisper, "— *with much less bloodshed.*"

She pulled back. Just far enough to watch as that intense focus of his shifted inward. She could actually feel him weighing his options—her.

As far as he knew, she was new to the military. To Public Affairs. As of yet, untested by both. Was she still more reporter than soldier?

It was a critical question.

Even if he decided to contact Captain Vaughn to officially, if confidentially, steer her away from General Ertonç—which he could do—Garrison had to believe there was a real risk that, if she did identify more as a reporter than a soldier, she might well pass on the tip to someone *not* beholden to Uncle Sam's military publishing dictates.

"Dessert."

Her confusion must've shown, because a low chuckle warmed the tiny space. His.

"Dinner. Tonight." He'd texted her his address before she'd even had a chance to pour her morning coffee. His eagerness hadn't surprised her. But the fact that the address wasn't the one she and Jelly had on file for him had. Even more surprising, the address he'd texted had come back not to an apartment, but a house.

When had he moved—and why?

"You're still coming over, yes?"

"Of course." For reasons piling up faster than she could count.

"Good. Give me a few minutes, and I'll see what I can do about your request to interview the general."

"And in exchange?" But she already knew.

"You don't put *me* on the record until after dessert."

This smile wasn't even scripted. "Deal."

Evidently she wasn't the only one fine-tuning her agenda. He was adjusting his as well. He'd accepted her story regarding her determined pursuit of the general's interview. Their dinner had simply provided him with an opportunity to pursue other, emerging, goals. An opportunity he wasn't above capitalizing upon. Specifically, his need to discern what she learned from said interview and intended to publish—as well as his own intention to control the information. And her.

She actually respected him for it.

But she still had no intention of letting him know he'd met his match.

Not even when his head dipped, bringing those intimidating shoulders too close for her peace of mind. For a moment, she was afraid he intended to push this meeting beyond the bounds of professionalism, but he finally paused, just shy of touching her.

His murmur warmed her ear much as hers had done his earlier. "Wait here."

With that, he straightened, turned around, and left.

She reached for her phone as soon as the door snapped shut, furiously typing the first in a slew of texts to her faux boss to aid in covering his ass along with hers, should Garrison stop to phone Captain Vaughn to verify the pertinent aspects of the story she'd just spun.

She'd been honest with Garrison. Partly.

Terry *had* asked for an interview with the general earlier that morning. He'd also been shot down. Though at the time, neither of them had known on whose authority the firm *no* had come. But Terry—loyal soldier though he was—was also very much a rabid reporter. The *no* had burned.

Hence, as she finished typing her final text, his response —*Understood. You owe me another bottle of vodka, but yeah, got your back*—wasn't surprising. Nor was his conclusion—*Now GET me that interview!*

Easier said than done. The door was still closed.

Regan stared at the walls of the tiny storage closet, its floor-to-ceiling shelves burdened with an assortment of audio-visual equipment, most high tech, but a surprising amount not. Silence resonated from beyond. Though she was tempted to slip into the lobby, she didn't. The captain had told her to wait here, so here she would wait. She wasn't opposed to following orders—even his—so long as they dovetailed into her *real* ones.

And if they didn't...

As the minutes began to multiply, she began to wonder—had Garrison gotten so tied up with his regular and newly added collateral duties that he'd forgotten about her? She caught the sound of steady boot falls in the lobby and tensed, not wanting to be caught by yet another Special Forces soldier, who would also be well within his rights to demand an explanation for her presence—or worse.

What if LaCroix had returned?

As the door opened and she spotted that leading enormous forearm, biceps and shoulder, she relaxed. The captain hadn't forgotten.

But had he managed the rest?

The door swung wide.

Garrison tipped his head toward the lobby. "Come."

That was all he said as he forged a determined path across the tiled expanse toward another, heavier door. This one led to a corridor with multiple wooden portals leading off the right. He stopped at the third one and opened it, tipping his head once more to let her know she should precede him inside.

She did. She found the general at the far end of a modest conference room, standing in front of its sole window and staring out between the open slats in the blinds, seemingly absorbed. With what, she had no idea.

Ertonç was oblivious to Garrison's "She's here, sir," as well as the subdued swish of the door that followed as the captain departed.

Once again, she was kept waiting.

A solid minute passed, during which she considered coughing to sever the man's attention from—what *was* he staring at so pensively?

She risked finding out.

Regan stepped around the wood-grained conference table and padded chairs taking up most of the room to join the general at the window. She immediately felt the intrusion. Hers. Evidently, she wasn't the only one suffering the jagged edges of memory and regret today. Thanks to the hours she'd spent last night researching this man, she even understood the ones rasping into him, as well as the cause of that telling sheen to his faded brown stare.

A male ACU-clad soldier stood in the grass roughly twenty yards away, scooping up a chortling boy of perhaps two or three. A young woman looked on, smiling, as the soldier swung the tot around and around before settling the boy jiggling belly down over his right shoulder. The soldier began laughing as well, causing the dampness in the general's eyes to finally well up and spill over.

She was about to step back and leave the general to his grief, when he stiffened.

"I'm sorry; I did not realize—"

"No, sir. It's my fault. I shouldn't have intruded. I'll wait outside."

"Nonsense. I invited you." He took a deep, cleansing breath as he scrubbed a leathery hand through short, steel-gray hair. "I was just—" He broke off as the hoarseness returned.

When he couldn't seem to gather the words to finish, Regan offered hers. "Remembering. I know. I understand you lost both your sons recently." In the same horrific car bombing outside Inçirlik, no less. She'd seen the photos. "I'm truly sorry for your loss, General." She wasn't sure if she'd gotten caught in the tangle of her own ancient memories—the ones that somehow managed to knot up her gut on this very day, year after year—or if it was the added knowledge of his, but she reached out and briefly pressed her hand to his forearm.

She wished she could offer more, but feigned Public Affairs or not, she dare not let on that she also knew that his wife had died from cancer two years before his sons were murdered. Or that his only daughter, an asthmatic, had had an attack and drowned in the ocean years before that while on break from her studies at a British university. Like her, this man had no one left on the planet.

Life just seemed to crap on certain people, didn't it?

Over and over again.

The general's sigh was heavy, resigned. "Yes, it has been a trying time. But I must move forward. Allah wills it."

She wasn't so certain of Allah's will, but she did subscribe to the gospel of pushing forward, and zealously. There were days, weeks even, when that dogged, forward momentum was all that got her through. That, and the Army.

"So, Lieutenant Pace—" He stretched his hand toward the conference table. "Shall we have a seat and begin?"

Regan ignored the unexpected twinge of guilt as she tacitly affirmed the phony name and rank with a nod. "Absolutely."

Military etiquette dictated she wait for the general to select his seat, which she did. She took the chair catty-cornered to the one he chose at the head of the table, retrieving her phone and turning on the microphone app before setting it down between them. She waited until he'd also settled his phone on the table beside him before she began.

"First, General, allow me to congratulate you on your recent promotion. I understand it's well deserved. I'm not sure you know, but my boss, Captain Vaughn, had hoped to interview you regarding the circumstances leading up to it, namely your role in Operation Peace Spring in northeastern Syria last year. You—"

"I am sorry, Lieutenant. You may ask me anything else you

like. But that topic is...how do you Americans say it? Ah, *off the table*." He softened the rejection with a smooth smile.

Clearly, he'd been prepared for the question. As he should've been.

But she'd had to try.

Regan mirrored his smile. "Of course. I apologize."

He inclined his silvery head.

"Moving on, then. Perhaps you could—" She broke off as his phone began to vibrate against the surface of the conference table.

His smile vanished as he looked down. Stared. Once again the man appeared to be transfixed, this time on the number currently displayed on his phone. An odd, almost cornered expression gripped his features as it vibrated a second time. He snatched up the phone—but not before she'd had a chance to scan the number herself and tuck it into memory.

"Excuse me a moment." He glanced pointedly at her own phone as he stood, tacitly ordering her to turn off her microphone. The moment she complied, Ertonç opened the connection on his and began speaking as he headed for the window. Quietly. In Turkish.

Interesting.

The country code fronting that call had been *German*.

He turned slightly, offering her an even more tantalizing view of his profile. The man couldn't seem to cease worrying his thick mustache with his fingertips as he spoke.

Who was on the other end of that conversation?

The general wrapped up the call all too quickly and headed back to the table, this time slipping his phone into one of the pockets on his camouflaged blouse as he sat. "I apologize for the interruption."

"No need, sir." She clicked the microphone back on, taking advantage of his lingering distraction as she opened with her most pressing question. "I understand you were originally slated to visit Hohenfels five weeks from now. Is there a reason why you've arrived so early?"

This smile was significantly less smooth than his earlier one. Because the question—or, more importantly, its answer—had unsettled him? Or because of that call and the distress still pinching his oddly blanched features?

Either way, he recovered quickly—and shrugged. "It was necessary."

"Necessary?"

He nodded. "There are many pressing matters to which I must soon attend in my country. Your post commander was gracious enough to accommodate my schedule by allowing me to move my visit and my speech forward."

It was a lie.

Even without Mira's insider knowledge, she'd have known that. The latest instinctive tug he gave his mustache proved it. Unfortunately, this was supposed to be a friendly interview, not an interrogation. She couldn't afford to press it.

"Why come to Hohenfels at all?"

"It was unavoidable."

"Unavoidable?"

"Yes. As you alluded to earlier, certain events have taken place in the world. Events that have...affected the way your army and mine relate to each other." *Syria. The safe zone.* Though he hadn't voiced the words, he did confirm them with a nod. "These events must not be allowed to tarnish our relationship. We are, after all, all soldiers. Subject to the policies of our respective governments. As you are no doubt aware, politicians come and go. Soldiers remain. Soldiers who must be able to truly and fundamentally trust one another, and be willing and able to work together again when called upon to do so, especially upon the battlefield. I am here to promote this."

Another tug on that mustache and another whopper. Worse, several of those lines had been lifted directly from the speech he'd just given.

Talk about recycling content.

Regan leaned forward to confront that faded stare head-on. "Working together? As in Kabul—where you and Captain Garrison first met?"

Score one for the captain's man Friday skills. Garrison had obviously briefed the general on the conversation they'd shared in that storage closet because Ertonç was ready for that one, too.

The general even managed a slight, almost genuine smile. "Yes, like Kabul. But that must be a story for another day." He stood. "I am sorry, Lieutenant. This is all the time I have for questions. I have a pressing meeting to attend shortly, and I must prepare. Would you like me to call you an escort?"

Foreign brass or not, she knew when she'd been deftly deflected—and decidedly dismissed.

With no choice but to obey, Regan scooped her phone off the table, ending the recording as she too came to her feet. "Thank you, sir, but I know the way. I appreciate your time and your patience with my questions. I hope you enjoy your stay at Hohenfels."

From the diffuse nod Ertonç offered, his mind was already elsewhere. As he retrieved his phone from his pocket before heading toward the window, she knew where his mind was focused, too—or, rather, upon whom.

Or she *would* know. Just as soon as she got out of there.

Ertonç had pulled up his calls log and hit redial on his most recently received one just before he'd turned.

Regan abandoned the man who'd already abandoned her, departing the conference room and heading down the hall to the lobby as quickly as she dared. Now was not the time to attract attention. Especially Garrison's.

Not with that number blistering through her brain.

The moment she cleared the main outer doors to the building, she punched in her fellow CID agent's number.

Jelling answered on the first ring.

"How's your son?"

"Fantastic. Appreciate your text earlier. I was so caught up, I forgot to answer. Sorry. But, yeah, they got his fever down, and we were able to bring him home a couple hours ago. He and Ava have been sleeping since. I was just getting ready to head into the office."

"That's a relief." And it was. But— "I need a favor, Jelly." One she actually preferred he do from the privacy of his home. "Don't leave for work just yet. You still tight with Mikel Gruber?"

"Yeah, why?"

She popped a salute as she approached a colonel on the sidewalk, then kept walking for several yards before shooting a quick glance behind her to ensure her six was clear of potential observers before she risked answering. "I need a local number traced, and I don't want the fact that I did it getting back to the post commander." Much less Garrison. At least, not yet. "The general took a call about fifteen minutes ago. One that's had him visibly on edge since. He's returning it now." Instead of preparing for his so-called pressing meeting. "It may be nothing. But my gut says otherwise. I think that call may be key to why he's really in Hohenfels." And *that* may impact LaCroix plans.

Which definitely impacted their case.

"Your gut's good 'nuff for me, Prez. Zap it to me."

Regan rechecked her six before quietly rattling off the digits she'd memorized at the start of the interview, then waited dutifully as Jelly repeated the string of numbers back. "Yeah, that's it."

"And I'm on it. But it may take a day or so before we get the information. I don't know if Mikel's workin' today."

"If not, step into him." With everything she'd learned during that speech and after, with both Garrison and the general, not to mention that blistering stare down, her gut was also telling her they didn't have days. Nor did Ertonç.

And where would their US-Turkish army-to-army cooperation be then?

Where would NATO's?

5

R egan brought the Tiguan she'd rented in Rachel Pace's name to a halt in front of Garrison and LaCroix's two-story picturesque timber and whitewashed stucco. Since the home's cobblestone drive afforded space for a mere two cars, and the captain's silver Wrangler was already parked on the right, she could only assume the slot on the left belonged to the pickup truck registered in LaCroix's name.

Which was missing.

Regan weighed her options for all of two seconds before pulling the Tiguan into the empty slot instead of parking politely behind the Wrangler. If she was lucky, the sergeant just might be annoyed enough to interrupt his housemate's date before she departed. And if he didn't?

Tonight might well be for naught.

That she couldn't afford. There was too much at stake. Namely, the general's life.

Meeting Ertonç and empathizing with his own shitstorm of a life, however unexpectedly, had made the coming hour and a half all the more urgent, even without NATO in the mix.

Regan killed the VW's engine and retrieved her phone from the passenger seat to text Mira. *okay, here. 90 min—not one second more.*

If she decided she was making worthwhile progress at that point, she could always signal to Mira that she needed to stay longer.

Her phone pinged with the woman's thumbs up emoji, followed by a smirking smiley face and a pithy *u can do this.*

Right.

She could. She had. This was standard op, nothing more.

So, go in there and make nice. Eat. Connect. Get what the Army needed—what her *country* needed—and then get the hell out.

Only that was the problem. There was nothing standard about tonight. As far as she'd been able to determine, the man she was about to dine with wasn't guilty of anything other than protecting a fellow—if foreign—officer. Worse, the captain was looking forward to their dinner. For added professional reasons, yes. But for him, tonight was extremely personal. He was a decent guy, too. Someone she might have eventually accepted a real date with had the circumstances been different.

But they *weren't* different.

Garrison was her only viable conduit to LaCroix.

The reminder didn't help. In fact, she'd never felt more like her father than she did right then. The irony twisted in as she tucked her phone in her back pocket before grabbing her trusty leather bag with its trustier, concealed metallic contents. She checked her watch as she bailed out of the Tiguan.

Eighty-eight minutes left.

Move out, soldier.

She ignored the stiff evening breeze cutting through her cable-knit sweater and jeans as she pointed her boots toward the cobblestone walk. Though the sun had set, there was enough lingering light for her to follow the path around the house to the main entrance.

The door opened before she could knock. Her date's daunting proportions crowded the frame.

Like her, Garrison had exchanged his uniform for a several shades darker, oatmeal-tinted sweater and jeans. Unlike her, the man had a checkered dish towel slung over his right shoulder—and a wide smile that was doing its damnedest to showcase that deep, dimpled fold.

"Hey, Rachel." He motioned her inside as he stepped back to allow her to enter. "Good timing. I'm almost done. "

She closed the door and followed him through the modest living room with its overstuffed couch and matching navy chairs. The archway near the end opened into a slightly larger and more modern kitchenette with an eat-in area on the near side of a stainless steel, granite-topped cooking island. "That smells fantastic. What is it?"

It wasn't an exaggeration. Her stomach actually growled at the pungent aroma.

"Sesame ginger beef." He rounded the island and began scraping a bamboo spatula in and around the interior of a large blackened wok as she stopped at the square table to hang her bag on one of the dark-red chairs. "I hope you weren't being polite when I texted about allergies and preferences."

"I wasn't. I'll eat pretty much anything I don't have to cook. And thanks for the GPS pin." Not that she'd needed it. She'd driven by the house after she'd rented the Tiguan that morning. After discovering he'd moved from the apartment complex still listed on his record, how could she not?

"No problem." The captain launched another open grin over the island. "I had a vested interest in getting you here."

That was what worried her. At least his mood was light. Whatever General Ertonç had reported back about their meeting, it couldn't have bothered Garrison. She'd take the win. Especially since she was still waiting—and none too patiently—on Jelling's back-door connection with the German phone company.

As for the address, "I'm surprised though." She tipped her head toward the living room. "I figured you for a studio bachelor pad. This is a lot of space."

"Yeah, it is—and I did have an apartment. But when my lease came up a few months ago, a local I'd met talked me into staying here and watching the place while he and his wife traveled." He shrugged as he refocused on the wok. "It's worked out okay."

"I'm glad." Regan slipped her phone into her bag and secured the zipper before heading for the counter and that amazing aroma drifting up from his efforts. "I might not be able to cook, but I'm good with plates and cutlery." She pointed to the row of stainless-steel cupboards attached to the wall behind him. "In there?"

He nodded. "Tea cups are to the left of the sink."

Tea? Yikes.

Beggars weren't supposed to be choosy, right? She'd save that for the information she desperately needed to elicit. Though not just yet.

But she did risk a, "For two? Or will your housemate be joining us?"

"Guest." He noted her arched brow and elaborated, "Evan's a guest. He and his housemate got into it last week, so I offered him a place to crash while he works a few things out. That said —" The captain shot her a decidedly satisfied smile. "He's out for the night."

She'd feared as much.

But his previous comment intrigued her. On several levels.

Could it be that simple?

If the sergeant was Garrison's guest—and not his housemate

—that affected LaCroix's legal status in the home. And his rights...and the tantalizing lack thereof. That information was well worth any disappointment over the sergeant's current absence.

Regan made a mental note to text Jelly about obtaining a copy of the lease on the house as she reached into the cupboard to withdraw a pair of cream plates and two small, handle-less Asian mugs from the door beside it. She headed for the table to arrange the plates and mugs on opposite sides, before returning to the kitchen proper to search for cutlery.

"Chopsticks are in the drawer on your left too. Unless you prefer—"

"No, that's good." She opened the drawer only to pause in mid-reach.

There was shallow woven basket near the back of the counter. Inside was a man's brown leather wallet. On top of that —a set of keys.

Garrison's, undoubtedly. But did one of those beckoning keys unlock the door to LaCroix's room, to be used in case of an emergency?

More importantly, *how* did she get—

"Rachel?"

Regan flinched as a hand engulfed her right shoulder. It fell away as she spun around, every cell in her brain and body instinctively on alert, whether she wanted them to be or not.

"Sorry. I didn't mean to startle you."

Shit. What the hell was wrong with her today? But she knew. She *was* on edge. Just not for the reason the captain assumed, let alone the reason she was willing to admit.

Humiliation singed her cheeks. "No, it's me. I just—"

"Don't really know me. This place. It's okay. I've been known to react instinctively to an unexpected stimulus too. Hell, a lot of soldiers do."

PTSD.

His bald honesty, not to mention the telling shadows threading into the compassion simmering in that stare, increased her humiliation.

She nodded. "Yeah. Well, with me, it's a...childhood thing." Mostly.

It wasn't as though she could admit to the rest. Not with being a freshly commissioned butterbar and all.

To her relief, he didn't push it. Instead, he carefully reached around her and retrieved two pairs of wooden chopsticks. The one's she'd forgotten all about.

"Here you go."

She accepted the slender offerings and escaped to the table, her humiliation skyrocketing as she spotted the pot of tea, bowl of rice and steaming wok he'd managed to lay out while she'd been standing there behind him, transfixed by the temptation in those keys.

She glanced at her watch. Seventy-one minutes left.

Time to get her head in the game. *Now.*

One good thing had come of her mortifying reaction. While the captain still pulled out the nearest chair for her, he kept his hands to himself for a change as she sat. He took the opposing chair and helped himself to some of the steamed rice, then held out the bowl. "By the way, I want to thank you for today."

"Isn't that my line?" She accepted the rice and spooned some onto her plate. "You are talking about the interview I needed?"

And she had needed it. Just not for the reason he believed.

That distracting fold cut in as he topped his rice with a generous portion of the fragrant stir-fry. "Trust me; you can still thank me." His smiled eased, his humor fading with it. "Seriously, though. The general's going through a rough time. He's taken some serious knocks. And, as you've also no doubt surmised, there's not a lot of sympathy for him on this post. For obvious reasons."

Which begged that rather critical question that still remained unanswered. Why was Ertonç even here?

She added some of the beef and vegetables to her rice. "And you? Do you have sympathy for him?"

"Yeah, I do. It's complicated. *He's* complicated."

So was the man sitting across from her.

And rapidly becoming more so. At least to her.

The captain was noticeably taking care to keep his hands to himself now, each time he passed something to her. As much as she wanted to resist appreciating the effort—and him—she couldn't.

"Anyway, he likes you. But I'm not supposed to tell you that."

She could only hope it would be the first of many revelations. Still, after the probing questions she'd posed that afternoon, upon which Garrison had definitely been briefed, she was surprised. "I just did my homework after my boss called me into his office. Learned a few things." Abused them.

The guilt still simmered over the latter.

Garrison's hand came up as he leaned forward. Slowly, as though she was a colt he feared might bolt—but, unfortunately, it still came. And he still wrapped those callused fingers around hers to squeeze gently. "It was more than that, and you know it. You connected with him when he needed it. From what he told me, you seemed affected too."

She had been. More than she wanted to admit—to Ertonç, the man sitting across from her, and herself.

Fortunately, the captain released her hand. She breathed easier as he focused on his food and dug in. She took a tentative bite, then a substantial one when the taste lived up to its scent. "This is *really* good."

He rewarded her honesty with a laugh. "Thanks." He leaned

forward to pour the steaming tea for both of them. "So, you got your interview with the big guy. You don't need to grill me anymore. At least about him."

"Oh, I don't know. There's a mystery or two left there."

"Really?"

She nodded. "How you both met, for one."

That damned dimpled fold cut in. She swore he'd intentionally weaponized it against her. "You mean you didn't ask him?"

They both knew she had. But she could play pretend, too. Better than he, in fact. She didn't have that lovely pulse point to rat out her true emotions. The captain really did *not* want to discuss this. Too bad. "As a matter of fact, I did ask. But it was at the end of our interview and he was in rush." She pushed forth a light shrug as she reached for her tea. "He left it to you to fill in the details."

They both knew it was a lie. Just as they both knew he couldn't afford to risk piquing her "reporter's" curiosity more than it already had been by calling her out on that lie.

He smiled instead—with nary a dimpled crease in sight. "Okay, then." He retrieved his tea, using the cup as she had. As a shield. "We met in Kabul. I was a first lieutenant at the time, dealing with a warlord who'd become a real pain in the Army's ass. I'd heard about a Turkish colonel who was tight with him." He nodded. "Ertonç. He also had a rep as an ass, but I probably did too, so it evens out. Anyway, I paid Ertonç a visit, did something to show due deference to the man, and he was impressed enough to make the intro I needed with the warlord. Even vouched for me." Garrison returned his cup to the table without taking a sip. "That's about it."

The hell it was. That vague little tale created more questions than answers and he knew it. "What exactly did you do for the general?"

Silence greeted that question, followed by an enigmatic shrug.

The shadows were back too. The complicated ones that clouded his stare with an intensity she wasn't comfortable with. For his sake.

Time to lighten the mood.

She tapped the rim of her cup and teased, "Tea? Aren't you supposed to woo a woman with fine food and a finer wine?"

Instead of easing, the shadows multiplied...and deepened. What on earth had she said now?

Unfortunately, silence greeted that unspoken question as well. She was contemplating the best way to break it when he offered up another one of those enigmatic shrugs. "I only drink when I'm depressed—*very* depressed—which I am definitely not at the moment. Besides," he reached for his own tea, toasting her with the cup as he made a visible effort to haul himself out of this latest, inexplicably murky quagmire. "I'm on call while the general's in town."

Of that, she was all too aware. But because of his collateral man Friday duties? Or did Garrison's previously admitted concerns for Sergeant LaCroix—and the *things* LaCroix needed to work out—play into his vigilance, too?

It was as good an opening as any. "Speaking of the general—" She retrieved her chopsticks and prepared a bite. "I saw something odd this morning."

"What's that?"

"A look. Just before that speech. Between you and your houseguest. It wasn't friendly."

"Ah, that. It was nothing. A work-related issue that's been settled."

Another lie between them. Nor did she need a telltale pulse to know it. It was in the sudden tension in his grip on that cup.

Instinct had her pushing it. Ruthlessly. "That's good, I

suppose. It's just— I've been thinking about the guy off and on today. Well, since that speech. I thought that, perhaps..." She trailed off deliberately, left the bait jiggling about for several beats before she shook her head. "I guess not."

Oh, yeah, she'd hooked him.

The captain actually leaned toward her, then stopped, holding himself rigid as he waited. Until, finally, "You thought what?"

"Carys." This time, she simply dropped bait in the water... and waited.

Confusion nibbled first. Then suspicion. And then, the bite. The one she'd been counting on. Full-on jealousy. "Carys? You spent the day thinking about *Evan* and his fiancée?"

"Yes and no. It was a weird morning. In several ways. When I arrived at the auditorium, I bumped into some sergeant. He mistook me for the woman. Called me by her name, in fact. He seemed stunned that I was wearing an Army uniform—until he realized I wasn't her. I guess... Well, I didn't realize I look so much like her. According to that sergeant, I'm her twin. You didn't tell me that last night." She tinged that last with hurt and more than a bit of accusation.

"Who was it?"

"The soldier?" She shook her head, added a furrowed frown. "I didn't catch his name. He was wearing an SF tab, though. Does that help?"

"Doesn't matter. He was probably with LaCroix in Syria last year. Hence, his surprise over your uniform. Carys was Scottish."

"You do know her then?"

"No. I was in Yemen when Peace Spring went down. I've never even seen a photo of the woman, so I have no idea how much she may, or may not, have resembled you." He reached up, his fingers catching a stray strand of her hair as his remaining jealousy ebbed beneath the clearly welcomed balm she'd offered in the form of her own vulnerability. He tucked the strand behind her ear. "Okay?"

"Okay."

He sat back, staring at her...and, yet, not. He appeared to be looking through her. He nodded to himself, as though something had clicked.

"What is it?"

"Hmm?" His vision cleared. Focused. He seemed surprised she'd read him so easily. "It's nothing."

It was definitely something. Someone. *LaCroix*.

Unfortunately, she'd pushed it as far as she could. For now.

"Besides, it wouldn't matter if I'd met Carys." He reached for the bamboo spoon in the wok to help himself to seconds.

"Why's that?"

"You're the only woman I've ever cooked for." He glanced at her plate, still burdened with her first serving. "Though I'm not sure you think it tastes as good as it smells."

"I do." She used her chopsticks to prove it. "The only woman, huh? I'm not sure I believe that."

"It's true. Well, except for Beth—"

"See?"

He reached out to tap her nose. "She's my sister; she doesn't count."

"Oh, I'm sure Beth will be happy to hear that." She was curious though. More than she should've been. "Older or younger?"

"Younger. By five years."

The affection in his voice made her envious. She'd always wanted a sibling. Perhaps more kids would've stopped her mom from checking out of the world the way she had. Though probably not. Her mom'd had bigger problems than an awkward, lonely child.

"Rachel?"

She glanced up from her still brimming plate. "Just dealing with my jealousy; I'm an only kid. Let me guess—Beth made up for the torturing she did when you were young by teaching you your mad culinary skills so you could impress women later in life? Not a bad trade-off."

He didn't laugh the way she'd hoped. If anything, her teasing had caused those murky shadows to return, along with an odd, palpable distance.

Her instincts zeroed in. For once, she wished they hadn't. She'd spotted a few of those particular shadows before—in that parking lot, last night. "Your sister's...okay, isn't she?" Carys certainly hadn't been.

If anything, the shadows intensified. But he sighed. "Yeah. She's good—now. For a long time she was lost to me though."

Lost? "As in...drugs?"

He shook his head. "Dead. Along with our mom. Or so I was told. Our folks divorced after Beth was born. I was five. Dad got the farm and me. My mom got her freedom and Beth. I guess my dad got sick of me crying for them because he finally told me they'd been killed in a car crash." His laugh was short and utterly devoid of humor. "He even managed to blame it on her. Said my mom hadn't belted either of them in."

"Jesus." That proprietary hand flashed through her brain. The one that had seated her in his car the previous night, then continued on to latch her belt. For her...or himself?

"Yeah. He was piece of work."

"How did...?" It was well past the bounds of why she was there tonight. But she needed to know. For herself—and him.

"How did I find out my sister was still alive?"

She nodded.

"My dad died. Tractor accident. I wasn't there. I'd joined the Army at seventeen. Had just made sergeant when I got the news. There was no way I was going back to Kansas, except to sell the place. While I was going through his papers, I found a bunch of letters from my mom, begging for information about me. She'd stopped writing when I was nine, but there were enough clues in them to start searching. By the time I found Beth, our mom had been dead for years. Beth was fifteen and living in a dump with a distant cousin I also never knew I had. I filed for custody the same day. The cousin fought it—for the social security benefits, I'm sure. But, as I said, I'd made sergeant, and as my legal dependent, Beth had access to Army schools and healthcare. I won."

"And Beth?"

"It took a while to win her over. But she pulled through, finished high school. Even went to college. Things are good. Beth married a buddy of mine last year. She's expecting their first."

"That's amazing." He was amazing. But he didn't see that. The pride in his face was all for his sister. Her jealousy returned, a hundred-fold. What would it have been like to have had someone like him in her corner?

She'd never know.

Hunger had fled. She reached for her now tepid tea to give her hands something to do. "She's lucky she had you. I can't imagine a parent doing that." And she'd had no prize-winners in that department herself. "How could he just...?"

"Pretend they were dead?"

She nodded. What kind of bastard did that? To his own son, no less. And for all those years? That seat belt flashed in again. It didn't even matter that Garrison had finally learned the truth; the damage had been done. To him and his sister.

"Who the hell knows? Lies just come easy to some people. It's their second nature." He sounded almost resigned to the thought.

"You haven't forgiven him, have you?"

"Hell, no." Another harsh laugh cut through the kitchen. This one as bereft of humor as the other, perhaps more so. "I haven't forgiven that man for a lot of things. But especially that." His appetite must've fled too, because he pushed his plate away. "Anyway...I have *no* idea why I just laid all that on you."

Silence thrummed between them. It should've been awkward, but it wasn't. It felt...natural. As did the need to reach out. Her fingers succumbed to the urge before she could stop them, and covered his.

"I'm glad you did."

He turned his hand in hers—and squeezed back. As she looked down at their fingers, his dwarfing hers as they lay on the table between them, now entangled, the panic that should've been there all along finally surged, and she jerked her hand away. The awkwardness set in then. With a vengeance.

They could both feel it.

"Would you like some coffee?"

"God, yes." Almost as much as she needed the physical reprieve from him and that dangerous contentment she'd just felt.

She held her breath as he stood and headed around the island, only letting the air escape when he was safely in the kitchen proper. She turned her attention to her plate. Her dinner was ice cold. Even if it hadn't been, she couldn't have finished it. Not while desperately trying to digest the dismay and the guilt.

Of all the men to have hit on her in that bar.

But what other choice did she have but to see this through? The stakes were too high to pull out now. She had to find a way to get to LaCroix and figure out what he had planned before the general ended up dead—and worse.

She risked a glance at the kitchen. At Garrison. He kept his massive back to her as he moved along the counter to fill the coffee maker with water and grounds before he set the machine to brew. Even after he finished, he still kept his back to her. As though he knew she needed the space. And with that towering frame, it was the only way he could give it without leaving the room.

Another wave of guilt churned in.

Why couldn't LaCroix have taken the damned bait? She'd have had no problem using the sergeant's attraction to further her case—or lying her ass off to him in the process. The mission was that important.

Dirty soldiers, or cops, *had* to be taken down. She had absolutely zero issues with being the one to do it. She never had. Garrison and his sister weren't the only ones who'd experienced firsthand what happened when life's traitors were left in place to soil and fester. Like them, she'd lived it.

"Here you go."

She flinched, nearly upending the steaming contents of the mug he held out all over the table and floor. She flushed for the second time that night. "Sorry."

He set the mug on the table. "I didn't know how you like it—black, white, sweet. I've got—"

"Black." Just as God and the Army intended. "Thanks."

He nodded, then sat. Stared. At her. With that same unnerving intensity he'd displayed the previous night. "You sure I didn't freak you out?"

"No."

He didn't appear to believe her.

She tried shaking her head for added emphasis, but that failed to dent the doubt as well. Would the truth? Did she dare?

"I... It's just—" She broke off. Moistened her lips as she searched for the courage to continue.

He waited, damn him. Gave her the same patience she'd given him on several occasions these past two days. Though his appeared to be born solely of genuine concern. Maybe that's what allowed her to actually voice it.

"It's...my dad. You weren't the only loser in the parental sweepstakes. He, ah— He was...killed."

"Oh, hon, I'm so sorry." He shoved their plates to the far side of the table and covered her hand with his. Again. But for some reason, the sight and feel of their intertwined fingers didn't have her pulling back. "When did it happen?"

Just as he had earlier, she laughed. And just as his had been, the sound was dark and stunted. Empty. "Nineteen years ago...tonight."

"*Christ*. And you chose to come over here and spend it with me?"

She'd had to. For so many reasons. Reasons she doubted he'd accept, even if she could tell him. Which she couldn't.

"If you don't mind me asking...what happened?"

For some reason she didn't. Even though she'd known it was coming. "He was...a cop."

"You said he was killed. In the line of duty?"

She opened her mouth. But as she stared into that unwavering intensity, she just...chickened out. Her courage had been used up. No matter how hard she tried, she couldn't seem to recharge it. And God help her, she actually wanted to.

"Rachel?"

Rachel. Not Regan. What the *hell* was she doing?

He didn't even know her real name.

She watched as his fingers came up to brush her cheek. She didn't flinch. Didn't even feel the urge.

But she did stand. Lie. "Yeah. Line of duty."

He remained in his seat as he blew out his breath. "That's rough."

He had no idea. No one did. Not even Mira. Not really. Her

colleague, her friend, who should have been calling her blasted phone right about—

What time was it?

More importantly, when had she stopped tracking it? She *always* tracked the time. On some assignments, minute by minute.

Maybe there was a God, because as she started to turn her wrist to peek, her phone rang. Its tone was unusually harsh and strident as it pierced the air, despite being tucked securely in her leather bag. Somehow she managed not to pounce on it. She even located a tight smile and pinned it into place.

"Excuse me."

He stood then, moving off to skirt the island as she unzipped the bag. Captain Vaughn's name scrolled across the screen as she retrieved her phone. Evidently she hadn't needed to take the precaution of assigning Terry's professional ID to Mira's number for the night. Garrison wasn't hovering over her shoulder as she'd feared.

"Yes, sir?"

Her friend's breathy rush filled the line. "I am *so* sorry I'm late. Please, please, *please* forgive me. I got called in. I'm inside the general's quarters now."

"Of course, sir. I understand." She waited several long beats, then continued, "Absolutely. I'll be right there."

Relief blistered in as she hung up and returned the phone to her bag before anchoring its strap over her shoulder. She would've turned to face Garrison as she crafted the words for her escape, but he was already beside her, disappointment tightening every generous muscle of that body as he stared down.

"Terry?"

"Yeah. He's got a lead on a story, and he's on a dinner date."

A wry smile cracked in. Briefly. "Go figure." The disappointment returned. "I'll see you to your car."

"No, you don't have—"

"I do." It was quiet. Adamant.

Before she could argue, that light, proprietary hand from the night before slipped into place at the small of her back, gently easing her along as they cleared the kitchen and the living room. She waited as he paused to open the front door to the house, then preceded him out onto the now-darkened porch.

Manners demanded she also wait for him to close the door, even as her every instinct ordered her to escape while she had the chance. *Run.*

Unfortunately, too much had passed between them at the table for her to obey. She stayed, even accepted the hand that settled back into place as he accompanied her down the cobblestone walk.

He was as good as his word, escorting her to her driver's door and patiently waiting while she retrieved the Tiguan's keys. But as she turned to offer her swift thanks and a swifter goodbye, the words clogged in her throat.

The night had closed in, shrinking the world down to just them, much as that tiny closet had that afternoon. But there were no uniforms now, no iron-clad Army regulations protecting her from the man who, yet again, towered over her. At five-eight, she wasn't short. But, Lord, he made her feel it.

He made her feel other things too. Things she didn't want to admit, much less act upon. But he did. It was humming in the air between them.

Expectation.

She ignored it. "Well, Captain. Thank you for dinner; it was fantastic."

He shook his head slowly. Firmly.

"Pardon? I don't—"

"John."

That patience he'd warned her about greeted her stubborn silence—and matched it.

Fine. She'd never get out of here otherwise. "John."

The tension spiked, along with that slow smile. That seriously distracting fold. She dragged her focus down, settling it on those three tattling scars that cut into his lightly whiskered jaw and neck. It didn't help. The pulse within was thrumming steadily, causing the tension to thicken.

Desperate to diffuse it, she reached up to trace the surprisingly smooth slivers of flesh, not for the first time wondering, "How did you get these?"

"Shrapnel."

Well, *that* she'd figured out on her own.

Of course, she'd had help discerning the cause of the thicker pair tangling down his neck, along with the endless, coarser rope that fed up his right arm, not to mention the dozen other scars she couldn't see because they were currently covered by his sweater and jeans. But his bronze star with V device for valor and twin purple heart write-ups hadn't mentioned this particular trio.

She was curious as to why.

He must have accepted that her patience and stubbornness matched his because, eventually, he offered a shrug. "Hindu Kush. I was still a kid. Stupid. Stuck my head up when I should've kept it down and nearly got it blown off. The shrapnel that ricocheted in served as a timely reminder to not do that again. After things cooled off, our medic pulled out the pieces and patched me up. The nicks had already started to close by the time we reached camp, so I never bothered with stitches." His hand found its home at the small of her back as he pulled her close. *Very* close. "Do they bother you? My scars?"

"No."

But he bothered her. And he shouldn't.

It was time to—

The thought burned away as that hand slid up her spine and smoothly drew her the rest of the way in. A split second later, his mouth was coming down to meet hers. Given his size, she would've expected him to bulldoze his way through the kiss that followed—would've been able to hold out if he had. But he didn't. He used his lips and his tongue to gently tease and torment until, before she realized what she was doing, she was stretching all the way up into the hard cocoon of his body, asking for more. John Garrison was one hell of an amazing kisser, and he tasted even better.

The eight o'clock whiskers beneath her fingers and palm dug in as he groaned and pulled her that much closer. Went deeper.

She didn't care. She wanted him to stay exactly where he was, continue doing exactly what he was doing. So much so, she actually protested and tried to draw him back when he stiffened, then straightened.

Why—

"Well, well. Looks like someone's inherited my taste for fresh meat."

LaCroix.

She couldn't see the man, of course. And it wasn't because of the dark.

It was John. He'd shifted as he'd straightened, those imposing shoulders now effectively shielding her from the sergeant's view. He didn't turn to face LaCroix. Nor did he speak. But the man's emotions were flat-out roaring their protest at the crude interruption. As her palm slid down to his chest, she could feel the fury as it thundered and rolled beneath. She could also feel him working to tame it, until suddenly it was gone, seemingly absorbed. Completely.

It wasn't until John had tucked her keys into her hand and

deftly guided her into the Tiguan's driver's seat that she realized he'd taken them from her to open the door. She felt more than heard the click of her safety belt as he latched it, and then his lips were brushing her temple and warming her ear.

"Drive safely. Text me when you get back to the Lodge."

Though gently murmured, it was an order. From the man she'd dined with tonight, not the combat-hardened captain who straightened and stepped back, patiently waiting for her to depart before he risked turning to confront his friend.

Except, she wasn't too sure about the friend part.

Not anymore.

As much as she wanted, needed, to stick around for the coming confrontation, Rachel wouldn't have. So Regan nodded obediently and started the engine as John shut the door. Regan also kept both men in her view for as long as she could as she backed the Tiguan out of the drive before ninety-degree reversing it into the street.

Just before she lost sight of the men, she caught the fury that lashed back in to permeate John's entire body just before it blistered free.

What the hell was he saying?

6

Regan was well into her second cup of morning coffee when her phone rang. Adrenaline kicked in, superseding her desperate need for caffeine as she spotted the number on the screen. It wasn't the call she'd been dreading since dinner had ended the night before; it was Jelly.

She snatched the phone off the tiny table in her room's kitchenette. "Morning, partner. Please tell me you got your hands on a copy of that lease."

"I did. And it says exactly what we want it to say—"

Yes!

"—but that's not why I'm calling."

Just like that, her euphoria burst. The apprehension in Jelly's voice had punctured it. That, and the distinctive rumbling of an engine in the background. A diesel engine. Jelly was in his SUV, driving while using his phone. Something the new paranoid papa in him was loath to do—even with the vehicle's hands-free feature.

"What happened?"

"Got a call from Mikel. That number you memorized off Ertonç's phone?"

"Yeah?"

"He's got nothin'—and it ain't for the lack of tryin'."

Shit. "Are you telling me that number came back to a burner phone?"

"Yep. Not to worry—at least not yet. Mikel's still digging. Let's just say, we've piqued the man's curiosity. He's triangulating the location of those two calls, and any others from that number, as we speak. I'll let you know what he finds out. Meanwhile, Mikel was able to give me the name of the vender who sold the burner." The diesel's rumble died out. Moments later, Regan caught the slam of Jelly's driver's door. "I'm in front of the kiosk in question now; it just opened. I'll call you when I'm out."

"Good luck. I'll be waiting."

Regan hung up. She was about to dump her phone on the kitchenette's table when it resumed trilling.

Once again, the number scrolling across the screen was a welcome one. And, once again, it traced back to one of her colleagues—Mira. "Hey, stranger. Fancy hearing from you. You sure you have the time to call me?"

"Oh, God, Rae. I am so sorry. I know I was late backing you up—"

"*Again.*"

Mira's sigh filled the line as she absorbed the hit. "You're right. First the bar, then your dinner. I got hit with an emergency change to the babysitting schedule—a double shift to boot. The general was nice enough about it, but I couldn't very well explain away a call to you while I was actively watching his back from *inside* his rooms. The second he went to the bathroom, I jumped; I swear. I just got off duty. I'm on my way to my rental car now."

Which would be why Mira hadn't been waiting impatiently for her at the Lodge when she'd arrived home last night, anxious to grill her about what had happened. "That's okay. I'll forgive you. Someday."

"Thank you. So, how'd it go? King Kong stop beating his chest long enough to give up anything new?"

"Maybe."

That argument in John's driveway flashed in as Regan retrieved her mug of coffee and took a sip. Damn Brooks and his intense paranoia. If he'd authorized the tail on LaCroix, they might've actually known what was said after she'd been forced to depart. As it was, she'd have to return to John's home to explore the lead—and risk a second course of stir-fry and the disconcerting dessert he'd served up afterward.

She didn't get it. Like Mira, she'd never been into gorillas. Worse, she swore this particular one knew her interest had been grudgingly gained. It was as though John had sensed her reluctance all along and had known he'd have one shot at changing her mind. And, damn him, he'd actually succeeded. Where did that leave her? Them?

This case.

Because she still had a job to do. From that tantalizing glimpse she'd caught of John and LaCroix squaring off, she was more convinced than ever that not only did the sergeant have vengeance seething in his heart, he was nurturing it.

The general's days were numbered, all right. Quite possibly, his hours.

"Rae?"

"Yeah?"

"I thought I lost the connection. You okay?"

Hell, no. "Absolutely." She polished off the contents of her mug and headed for the sink to rinse it out. "Just waiting for the caffeine-fueled focus to kick in."

"So...what did you get?"

"A fresh angle." One that could just crack this case wide open

—*if* she could get Brooks to agree. "But first, I just got off the phone with Jelly. We hit a snag with the Ertonç number; it connects to a burner. Stay tuned though. Jelly's source is still on it. As for the angle, we got a positive hit regarding John's current digs. Jelly scored a visual on the lease to that house. John signed it—but LaCroix's name is not on it. Anywhere." Meaning that while she couldn't search the sergeant's room without permission and have it stand up in court, John *could*. "Also, they nearly came to blows last night as I was leaving. If I can get Brooks to let me bring him in on this, I think John might agree to search—"

"*John?*"

Crap. She really did need that coming jolt for focus.

Regan turned to press her suddenly pounding forehead into the front of the refrigerator. It didn't help. "Yes, John. That's his name."

She heard Mira's car door slam—but unlike Jelly's, this engine didn't fire up. "I know that's his name. But you don't *call* them by their names. Not the first ones."

"That's not true. I've gotten cornered into it before."

"Not when they're not around."

That was true.

Trapped, she went on the attack. "Why'd you call me anyway?" If Mira was in her car, she hadn't been home to decompress yet. Shower. Eat.

Sleep.

"Fine. We'll discuss *John* and what he might do in a minute. But first—I just got a call too. Kevin Walsh."

Regan pulled her forehead from the fridge and turned around to lean back against it. "Your SEAL buddy?" The one who'd provided Mira's initial intel on LaCroix's deteriorating attitude? An attitude that had gotten so bad it had apparently led to the sergeant getting kicked out of his apartment last week.

"Yeah. Kev just surfaced from his latest mission and got my message about Ertonç. Like Garrison, he dealt with Ertonç when he was still a colonel in Afghanistan, though roughly three years later than your captain. According to Kev, there's some seriously foul blood between Ertonç and the Kurds. He loathes them."

No stunner there. "A lot of Turks do." Hence the blood-letting establishment of that so-called Syrian safe zone.

"True. But Kev got the feeling Ertonç's disagreement was personal. How personal, he doesn't know. Just that Ertonç would shut folks down—and harshly—if anything even remotely positive about the Kurds came up in discussion."

Now that was interesting. It also begged the question: did Ertonç hate Kurds with the standard, all-too-common Turkish disdain...or was there something more specific to his hatred? Say, a particular cause?

More importantly, did that hatred have anything to do with the reason his sons were targeted for death by the PKK in that car bombing the year before?

Before she could pose the query to Mira, her phone beeped. "Hang on. I've got another call coming in." She pulled the phone away so she could check the number.

Jelly?

That was quick. Hopefully, not because he'd been shut down at the kiosk.

"Hey, Mira—it's Agent Jelling. Can you hold?"

"Just hang up and take it. That's all I've got. I'll check in after I've grabbed a nap."

"Sounds good. Sleep tight." Regan braced herself as she pulled her phone from her ear once more, this time to click over. "Good news?"

"Dunno. You tell me."

No engine rumbling in the background on this call. Meaning

Jelly had scored—but the results were too startling for distracted driving.

Oh, Jesus.

John.

It was the only scenario that made sense. She took a deep breath and just said it. "Captain Garrison bought that phone."

"Yep. Got the clerk's confirmation on the photo I showed him —not that we needed it. Don't know too many other talking mountains with that distinctive collection of scars lumbering about town, in uniform or not. But that's not all. The entire ID took ten seconds tops. The remainder of the time, I was fielding another call from Mikel. I forwarded the full report to your email, but the two calls you overheard in that conference room? They're the only two calls that phone has made, and both occurred at the same spot. I'm not sure you're gonna like the location—Klinikum Sankt Joseph."

A hospital?

Well, that didn't bode well, did it? "Jelly—"

"Hang on, Prez. I need a sec."

"No problem." It wasn't as though she had somewhere to be.

She could hear Jelly distancing the phone from his mouth as he rolled down the window of his SUV to greet someone in German.

Regan turned to frown at the close-up photo of a Bavarian pretzel featured on the monthly calendar attached to the wall as she waited for Jelly to resume their conversation. Saint Joseph's. Was Ertonç ill?

Was that why the general had moved his visit forward by a good five weeks? Had a difficult-to-secure appointment opened up? His body language when he'd taken that call had been unusually guarded. Not to mention, returning that call had been the first thing he'd done once he'd dismissed her.

Before she'd even left the room.

If Ertonç was ill, was he trying to hide his failing health from his chain of command? Possibly to preserve his career? It did appear to be all the man had left. If so, it could also explain why John had purchased that phone.

"Okay, I'm back. Apparently, I'm parked in the wrong spot. But I managed to badge my way out of the ticket."

"Excellent. Just don't tell Brooks." Their CO had enough reason to whale on her partner. "But about the calls—" Regan headed out of the kitchenette into the bedroom proper. "Could Mikel tell if they came from a particular area of the hospital?"

Regional medical facilities often covered a lot of real estate. Especially one that treated as many patients as the Klinikum Sankt Joseph. She'd take any help she could get in narrowing down the search radius.

"Yeah, that's the part you're not gonna like. Western-most wing. Only thing there is oncology."

"Cancer?" Well, crap.

As much as she hated to admit it, it fit. The general's features had been drawn during that speech and again during their meeting. In light of those moments at the window, she'd chalked up his wan appearance to a fresh bout of grief. What if there'd been another cause? One that had driven home his loneliness and sorrow as he stared out at that soldier and realized that, no matter how much he'd already lost in his life, he was about to lose even more. This time, *his* life. Whether she was able to thwart LaCroix's plans or not.

Either way, she was wrong about having nowhere else to be.

"Prez?"

Regan stopped in front of her closet to retrieve Rachel Pace's camouflaged uniform, tossing the ACUs on the still-rumpled covers of her bed. "I'm here. Do me a favor? When you get to the office, tell Brooks I may be awhile."

"Will do. You headed where I think you're headed?"

"Yup." Klinikum Sankt Joseph was half an hour away. She might not have an appointment. But there was an excellent chance Ertonç did.

FORTY-FIVE MINUTES later and a mere fifteen seconds after turning into the hospital's main parking lot, Regan had even more proof that the burner phone was connected to John. It was attached above the left rear bumper of the silver Wrangler parked three feet to her left: a Kansas plate. John's Kansas plate.

He was here, in this hospital.

Intriguingly, General Ertonç was not. Not unless there'd been a last-minute change of plans.

The moment she'd hung up with Jelling, she'd texted Mira about the general's schedule. Ertonç was locked into back-to-back meetings at Hohenfels, then Vilseck, until sixteen hundred that afternoon.

So why was his US Army liaison here at the *klinikum* and not at his side?

Arranging last minute details for the general's appointment? Or was Ertonç's health worse than she'd feared? Had John arrived in advance to prep the hospital for a pending VIP admission?

John was right; she had connected with Ertonç during those raw moments in the conference room. More than enough to sincerely hope he was okay.

Time to find out.

Uncertain as to what awaited her inside the building, Regan opted to drive the Tiguan into the adjacent lot, taking care to park in a slot that wasn't visible from the Wrangler or the path John would naturally take when walking back to it. With Rachel Pace's headgear firmly in place, she bailed out of the car and headed straight for the ER's main doors. She'd canvass the *klinikum* floor by floor if she had to, but she would locate John—and *then* she'd decide if it was prudent to reveal her own presence to him.

Success came sooner than she'd thought, and exactly where she'd feared.

Oncology.

Regan stepped out of the elevators and immediately faded into the antiseptic corridor off her right, edging back deep enough to ensure John couldn't see her—not that he was looking.

The captain stood twenty feet away, on the opposite side of the central-hub nurses' station from where that call had originated. Unlike her, he wasn't bothering to keep a low profile. It would've been difficult if he'd wanted to. Not only was John also in ACUs, he was deep in conversation with a dark-haired, lightly bearded Middle Eastern male sporting a white physician's coat.

Curiously, she had the distinct impression that John and the doctor knew each other, and well. Though they looked to be roughly the same age, the doc was at least half a foot shorter and a good hundred pounds lighter than the captain.

Both appeared unfazed by the inequity as they stood toe-to-toe, locked in a polite, though seemingly fundamental, disagreement.

Even more curious, John appeared to be losing.

Regan could feel his frustration from where she stood. He was doing his damnedest to keep it hidden, as he had the night before with his anger with LaCroix before she'd driven away. But hints were bleeding through, mostly in the faint tension in his shoulders and jaw. Though she wasn't close enough to verify, she suspected that telling pulse of his was clipping along at a daunting pace.

What *were* they discussing?

Even if she'd been close enough to catch more than every tenth word, she wouldn't have known. The men weren't conversing in German, English or Turkish, near as she could tell. According to the captain's record, John was also fluent in Pashto, Arabic and Farsi. They didn't appear to be using those either.

Whatever the language—and subject—John refused to give up. He dipped his head as he made another seemingly earnest attempt at persuading the doctor, but the man held firm. Another longer and frustratingly quiet comment from John, and the doctor finally appeared to weaken.

Several more earnest comments followed before the doctor's grudging nod signaled his surrender to...what?

She was contemplating brazenly heading over when one of the nurses at the station glanced up from her phone and politely interrupted the men.

Regan opted to inch closer instead.

Unfortunately, her street-gleaned German didn't include medical jargon. She was able to catch the doctor's name, though.

Karmandi. She'd heard it before...but where?

Karmandi responded to the nurse in German and turned to John, switching back to whatever language they'd been using as he appeared to make his apologies before turning to head down the opposite corridor.

Now what?

Brazen was still her best bet. Given the ticking bomb attached to the case, and quite possibly the general's life, it was her only bet.

Retrieving her phone from her trouser pocket, she opened her text app to a stateside friend's innocuous conversational stream as she strode, seemingly absorbed, out from her secluded spot and around the nurses' station—smack into John's titanic back.

He spun about, his hands shooting out to engulf her arms as he steadied her. "*Rachel?*"

"John?"

Pure, unabashed pleasure flooded his features. "What are you doing here? This is a—" Fear punched to the fore as the realization of precisely where they were drove home. Panic joined in as John's gaze swept her from head to toe, searching for something he clearly did not want to find—broken bones, bruising, blood.

Relief followed as he found none, only to evaporate when confronted with the reality that if she'd had an accident, she'd have gone to sick call like any other soldier at Hohenfels. She wouldn't be here, thirty minutes away, at the Klinikum Sankt Joseph. On *this* floor.

"This is the cancer ward. Are you...okay?"

It was her stomach's turn to knot as she felt his panic return. Surge. She was going to hell. That revealing catch in his voice had sealed it.

She pushed the guilt aside. "Of course. Why wouldn't I be?"

"Because you're here." Just like that, his demeanor shifted one hundred eighty degrees as professional overtook personal. "If you're okay, *why* are you here? Now?" Suspicion shredded his remaining concern. "Are you following me?"

Brazen. She had to see this through.

She'd caught the sergeant's expression last night along with John's as she'd backed out of his drive. LaCroix was ready to blow. Given his skills, that was a particularly dangerous state for the man—and General Ertonç.

"Why would I be following you?"

"I don't know. But if you're not, what could possibly bring you here?"

"My story."

His stare darkened, sharpened. "The general?"

She nodded. "I'm following a lead." She pushed a light shrug to the fore, damning herself that much more. "Well, more of a loose end. Either way, I need to get it tied it up before I can file my article." She held up her phone. "The general had his on the table during our interview. A number came across the screen during a call. I, ah, have this thing for numbers."

"A thing."

"Hmm. I see them once, and I remember them." Even upside down and sideways. "It comes in handy in my line of work." She could only hope he never found out just how handy. "I didn't realize it at the time, but I'd scribbled the number in the margin of the draft I showed Captain Vaughn. He asked, so I told him where it came from, and that the call had unsettled the general. Vaughn was curious too. He said I should follow up, see where it led. And it led—"

"Here."

It wasn't enough. She could still see the tension lingering in the press of John's lips, that nearly imperceptible lock to his jaw. Not surprising, since he knew damned well that the phone was a burner.

"How did you trace the number?"

"Oh, that was easy. I didn't." She waved her phone once more, before tucking it in her cargo pocket. "Captain Vaughn has a contact with a local phone company. The guy came through with the information this morning. Unfortunately, all he could provide us was the location of the calls. I'm still not sure why there wasn't a name on the line, but I figured what the heck, I'd stop by and see if anything stood out. I guess it did—" She nudged a smile laced with warmth and more than a bit of infatuation to her lips. "Because I found you."

The remaining tension eased. He'd bought it.

Time to switch tactics, before he changed his mind. "So, why are *you* here?"

Just like that, another instant, one-eighty shift. This one, defensive. The quintessential man who'd been caught in the act. If there wasn't so much at stake, it would've been amusing. But there was, and it wasn't.

How to get him to admit it?

Brazen.

"John...does General Ertonç have medical issues? Is that why he's really in Hohenfels? And why he arrived so early? Does he need treatment?"

"No." That was it.

It was enough. Not a single micro-expression flitting across his face betrayed that succinct response. John was telling the truth. But there was something else threading through his features. Relief. She was close enough to gauge that telltale pulse now too. Its normal, sedate pace had spiked. John might not be lying, but he was concealing something. Something big.

Before she could press him further, his phone pinged.

"Just a sec." He retrieved the phone from his pocket as he turned away, using those irritatingly hefty shoulders to shield the screen as he checked his text app. A split second later, his pulse skyrocketed.

"What's wrong?"

Preoccupation and worry overshadowed his smile as he turned back, the app already closed. The number on that sent text, gone. "Just a minor snafu." He might've been telling the truth before, but he was lying his ass off now. "I'm sorry, Rachel. I have to go. But I'd like to finish this conversation. Tonight? We never did have dessert."

The hell they hadn't. But she did need another crack at getting inside LaCroix's room, with or without John's assistance. Or knowledge.

She matched his terse smile and raised him a nod. "Sure."

"Great. I'll call you."

Her subsequent nod went unseen, at least by John. He was already striding around the nurses' station. The younger nurse stared after him, pensively tracking his determined movements as he passed the dormant elevator to take the stairs.

The nurse who'd spoken with that doctor.

Karmandi. Numbers she remembered. Names, not so much. But that one, Regan knew she'd heard before, and recently. To discern when and where, she'd need a first name. Fortunately, that was easy enough to get.

Regan stepped up to the counter as the younger nurse sighed and turned back. "*Entschuldigen Sie, wie lautet Doktor Karmandis Vorname?*"

"Olan."

Hmm. No reaction from the recesses of her brain. She smiled her thanks regardless and turned to follow the captain's path around the station.

Like John, she ignored the elevator. Her boots echoed as she entered the stairwell to descend the concrete steps...and only *her* boots.

Whatever had been in that text of John's, it must've been serious enough to have caused him to descend at double-time, because he was gone.

Despite the phone burning a hole in her pocket, Regan forced herself to wait until she reached the *klinikum's* main ER doors. Only when she spotted John's silver Wrangler pulling out of the lot, did she retrieve her phone and punch in her fellow CID agent's number.

Jelly answered on the first ring. "Whatcha got?"

No idea. Yet. "Do me a favor—open your laptop and run the name Olan Karmandi though your case file research and tell me what pops." Something would. She was sure of it. But what?

"That with a 'K'?"

"Yes." She'd run across it recently, all right. And in print. Because she could see the spelling in her head.

"Give me a sec. I'm not at my desk."

Jelly's off-key whistling filled her ear as she headed for her Tiguan. She had barely unlocked the driver's door and slipped inside when Jelly's whistling sputtered, then died a violent death —strangled by his curse.

His subsequent calm, "Hey, Prez, where'd you get that name?" gave her more pause.

"Here at the *klinikum*. He's a doc in oncology. I just watched Garrison hash something out with the man. I don't know what. Why?"

"'Cause the name's Kurdish. But that's not all. It's also the last name of the PKK terrorist who took credit for that explosion in Inçirlik last year. *Royar* Karmandi rigged the bomb that took out both the general's sons."

Holy shit. That's where she'd seen it.

Were Olan and Royar related?

Even if they were—*especially* if they were—why was John meeting with the doc? More importantly, why had Ertonç sent John here on his behalf? Because Ertonç had sent him. Those phone calls in the conference room all but proved it. Not to mention John's purchase of that phone in the first place, along with his body language with the general up on the stage—and at dinner in his kitchen last night. John hadn't lied. He did respect Ertonç. So much so, he'd come to the *klinikum* in the general's stead.

To do what? Negotiate?

It was the only scenario that made sense. Backchannel overtures were common enough in both geo-political and military arenas. Hell, in light of the volatile natures of war and detente, those overtures and the equally classified conversations that followed were often essential.

This one fit right in.

General Ertonç had known John for years and obviously trusted him. John also clearly knew the doc. And there was John's branch. If there was an overture to make, a Special Forces soldier was a solid choice to make it. It would also explain John's proactive protective posture toward the general, as well as his secrecy regarding that posture. It could even explain John's deteriorating relationship with his houseguest, Sergeant LaCroix. *And* his purchase of that burner phone.

But something was missing. Something critical.

Why would Ertonç even want to broker a deal—any deal—with a Kurd, let alone a Kurd possibly related to the one who'd taken credit for murdering both his sons? And did that rationale have anything to do with LaCroix?

"Prez? You still there?"

"Yeah." Just distracted. Seriously so. "Jelly, can you—"

"Run Olan through the system and see what comes back?"

"You read my mind. Dig deep. I want everything you can find on the doc. Where he lives, who he sleeps with, and how often. Hell, I want to know what brand of toilet paper he prefers, and how much he pays for it. But I *especially* want to know if he's related to our good friend Royar."

"I'm on it."

"Also, let Brooks know I've got another date with the captain lined up for this evening. Until then, I'll be holed up at the Lodge."

The irony bit in. A mere hour ago, she'd planned on heading into CID and hitting up Brooks with yet another request for a tap and tail on LaCroix. And when Brooks refused—which, in light of her serious lack of progress in the hard evidence department, he would have—she'd planned on going all out on the alternative: a request that she be allowed to bring John in on the case. Given the scene she'd witnessed in the captain's driveway last night, it might've worked.

Not now.

Not after learning that John had purchased that burner.

Not until she was absolutely certain she knew why he'd bought it—and could prove it.

She was forced to agree with Books' caution. Her gut might still maintain John's innocence when she could tell that even Jelly had begun to doubt it, but it wasn't enough. She refused to wager a man's life against her instincts.

Much less NATO.

So it was back to the Lodge. She'd go through every single sentence she and Jelly had been able to amass on Ertonç, LaCroix and the captain while she waited for the Karmandi info to tumble in. If she could prove John was serving as a backchannel, she just might be able to force her boss' hand— and get Brooks to agree to pull John in.

If not, she was headed back to that house. One way or another, she was going to get what she needed to put this investigation to bed.

Tonight.

7

Regan stared at the second hand as it completed yet another silent sweep around the face of the wall clock hanging in her kitchenette at the Sunrise Lodge. Another ten minutes and it would be eighteen hundred on the dot. The time John had suggested for the first dinner they'd shared. What the devil was taking him so long to confirm their second?

Relief seared in as her phone pinged. But as she grabbed it, she spotted the notification on the screen. The text wasn't from John; it was from Jelly.

Have confirmation—Olan & Royar are 1st cousins!

details in email

Adrenaline surged, despite that clock and its taunting time.

She dumped her phone on the kitchenette table and scanned the English-language Turkish newspaper still open on her laptop. According to the year-old article she'd pulled up, Olan Karmandi had not only denounced terrorism in general— and the PKK in particular—while still an undergrad, he'd also logged a serious slew of hours volunteering at a Turkish free clinic during medical school and after. Doctor Karmandi had doubled down on his views for the article's author, reiterating his horror and disgust with the PKK's tactics in light of the car bombing that had killed then Colonel Ertonç's sons days earlier.

When she added that to those calls with Ertonç—and John's physical intercession between the two—it was the proof she and Jelly had been waiting for. They could now connect Royar and the PKK to Olan, and from there, Olan to General Ertonç through John. And, of course, Ertonç to the Turkish government. But would it be enough for Captain Brooks?

Moments later, Regan had her answer as her phone pinged yet again. This text wasn't from Jelly. It was from Brooks.

spoke to Jelling—no go on Garrison
get him to confide in YOU!

Regan slapped her phone onto the table. Good Lord, was Brooks really waiting for John to spontaneously cop to a backchannel negotiation?

That was *not* going to happen.

She might not have known the man long, but she'd gotten to know him exceptionally well these past few days, especially after having spent the better part of the afternoon reviewing everything she and Jelly had been able to gather on him—including that heart-wrenching material in the background investigation conducted prior to John's top-secret clearance.

Until now, she'd thought the three years she'd spent with her grandfather following her mother's suicide had been rough.

She'd been stuck in Disneyland by comparison.

The statements in that BI from John's elementary teachers painted far too detailed a picture for her peace of mind. A broken right forearm, three cracked ribs, a not-so-mild concussion, along with countless sprains, welts and bruises—all before John had reached ten. She better understood his fundamental disdain for lies too. Not only had he grown up with that heinous one regarding Beth and their mom, he'd been forced to regurgitate the filth his dad had fed social services.

According to Earl Garrison, John had fallen out of a tree, gotten kicked by a vicious horse, and run smack into a five-foot commercial tractor tire he hadn't seen until it was too late.

The bastard's tales had been nothing if not creative.

Of course, no explanation had been volunteered by father or son when John had suddenly sprouted taller than his dad in junior high and begun to play football with an innate agility that'd stunned the hell out of his coach. Not a broken bone or a welt in sight from then on.

Regan had her suspicions as to how that final confrontation had gone down with dear old dad.

In the end, the information in that BI had only cemented what her gut had been insisting since those revealing moments in that storage closet. John might've been baptized into evil, but he'd consciously and consistently turned his back on it since. Those old-fashioned manners of his that had initially driven her nuts weren't an act, let alone a polished effort to get her into bed. They were an innate rebellion against the monster who'd raised him, a deep-seated effort at rising above.

There was no way John would be spilling military or geo-political secrets, backchannel or not. Not to her. Not to anyone.

Nor would he simply blow her off. Not willingly.

If John had changed his mind about pursuing a painfully green public affairs officer who stuck her nose in where it didn't belong, at the very least he'd have called to let her know.

Regan glanced at that damning clock. Eighteen hundred exactly.

Something had happened.

But did it have to do with that mysterious text John had received at the hospital? His beneath-the-radar negotiations for General Ertonç?

Or had his deteriorating relationship with Sergeant LaCroix finally come to blows?

The ringer on her phone grated against the quiet in the room, along with her increasingly excoriated nerves. She snatched her phone from the table, disappointment cutting in as she glanced at the readout. *Mira.*

"What's the word?"

"Still waiting."

"He hasn't even texted?"

Regan raked her fingers through the dyed strands of Rachel's hair, pushing the loose waves behind her shoulders. "No. And to answer your next two questions, Brooks says no on bringing John in on the case and an even louder no when Jelly reiterated our request to put a tail on LaCroix."

Yes, the sergeant was Special Forces. And, yes, if anyone had eyes in the back of his head, an SF soldier did.

Still, she'd managed to hold her own with John. So far.

She had worried that he'd begun to doubt her story after he'd departed the hospital that morning. But he hadn't so much as texted Terry to verify her claims about that phone number search. She'd checked.

So why hadn't John called, damn it?

Regan caught the distinctive whir of a microwave kicking in on Mira's end.

"Have you figured out how you're going to get into LaCroix's room?"

She drummed her fingers on top of the table. "Not a bloody clue." As attractive as those keys of John's were, breaking and entering was illegal. Faced with exigent circumstances, she'd do it in a heartbeat. The hell with it standing up in court. But she wasn't there—yet.

Worse, with Brooks' no-go still in effect regarding her

coming clean with John about LaCroix, there was no way she could risk asking him to search his guest room for her.

The microwave ceased its whir with a loud *ping*. "Rae—" She heard Mira open the oven. "Are you certain Garrison's loyalties are still sound? He did buy that burner."

"I know. And, yes." As many times as she'd done this, she ought to know. And that was before she'd absorbed the childhood horror detailed in John's BI.

"Then trust your gut. You're in the trenches, not your boss. If you think you need to bring the captain in, do it. When all's said and done, Brooks will be forced to back you up; you know that. For what it's worth, my instincts are in sync with yours. I've seen the guy a number of times these past few days—all of them with the general in the room. Those two have serious history, but it's not the sort that has Ertonç in danger. Not from Garrison. I can feel it."

"I know."

"So...what are you going to do?"

Brazen. This morning it had been the only path. It still was. "I'm going to drop by. Now. Because, well, come to think of it, John must've said, 'Dinner—same time, same place,' *unless* he phoned to say differently."

Mira's soft inhalation filled the line, followed by the thick silence of caution. "You sure? If you push it too hard, it might blow up in your face...and his."

They both knew what Mira wasn't saying. It just didn't matter. It couldn't. Only the case did. The general's life. NATO.

"I appreciate the concern, but I don't have a choice." When all was said and done, whatever she and John had managed to forge these past few days was destined to implode anyway. She'd realized that at the same moment she'd accepted that, somehow, he'd managed to well and truly get under her skin.

A swift glance at that taunting clock made her that much

more determined. "If I leave now, I can be there by eighteen thirty."

A good half an hour past last night's invitation, but close enough for her to blame her tardiness on yet another impromptu assignment from Terry.

She was going to owe the man a crate of vodka by the time this was done.

"Rae...what if LaCroix is there? If the two of them have gotten into it again, that could explain Garrison's silence."

That was what she was most afraid of.

Regan channeled the growing unease into action, eyeing her mist-green sweatshirt, faded jeans and running shoes as she stood.

Not exactly date-wear.

Too bad. They'd have to suffice.

She grabbed her bag from the back of the chair, double-checking that her most important accessories were still securely hidden within.

Satisfied, she slung the strap over her shoulder and departed the room. Within seconds, she was in the adjacent, darkened parking lot, unlocking the Tiguan and slipping into the driver's seat before she could change her mind. "I'll be fine. But stand by. If I need an out, I'll use John's bathroom to text you." He knew she had a girlfriend in town, the one she'd been waiting on in the bar that first night. "I'll tell him you got dumped and need a shoulder to sob on."

"Gee, thanks."

"What are friends for? Wish me luck." She hung up, hit the VW's lights and started the engine before Mira could do just that, lest the woman jinx her.

Fifteen minutes later, Regan turned the car into John's drive, once again parking beside his Wrangler. LaCroix's truck was missing.

One worry negated.

Unless the sergeant had already come and gone—violently.

She killed the lights and bailed out into the dark to skirt the front of the VW. She laid her palm on the Wrangler's hood.

The metal was stone cold. John had been home for a while.

So why hadn't he called?

The tension gripping her gut ratcheted tighter as she unzipped her leather bag—just in case—and stepped onto the walkway that led around the house. The tension eased a bit as she cleared the corner and reached the living room's main window. The blinds were drawn, but the slats were open. Though the table lamp beside the couch was switched to low, there was enough light for her to make out the distinctive white tee shirt and denim-clad form looming within.

John.

Unfortunately, her relief was supplanted by a fresh bout of unease that quickly morphed into dread as she headed for the door. She'd also spotted a bottle of whiskey on the coffee table. By John's own admission, he only drank when depressed. *Very* depressed. The bottle was open...and half empty.

She gathered her nerve, and knocked.

Reddened eyes greeted her as the door swung wide.

"*Fuck.*"

Instinct had her slipping her fingers into her bag as she stepped back.

"No!" John's left hand shot out—the one not dwarfing a squat glass of sloshing amber—to snag her arm. "Please. It's not you. I just realized I forgot to call. To reschedule."

Regan eased her fingers from her bag, the 9mm still firmly secreted within as she allowed John to draw her inside the house.

She waited patiently as he closed the door. But instead of facing her as the latch clicked, he turned to cross the room. He stopped beside the coffee table, raised the tumbler in his hand, and polished off the remainder of the whiskey within.

He bent down to set the glass on the table, then straightened and slowly faced her. "It's okay. I just had the one. I'm not drunk."

"I know." His path to the table had been straight and unwavering, the hand he'd used to drain that glass before setting it down, rock steady.

But something was wrong. Horribly wrong. Those dark gray eyes weren't red and swollen from booze, but grief. He'd been crying.

"What happened?"

"What else? Another goddamned bombing in the world. This time, Iraq." His grimace was short and stiff. "Big shock, eh?"

"I've been tied up. I hadn't heard." She slipped the strap of her bag off her shoulder and let it slide down to the charcoal rug beneath her feet.

"S'okay. The fallout hasn't made the news yet."

But it wasn't okay. Not for him. She stepped forward. "Who died?"

"An SF officer. Dan Stoeble. He'd just made major. Fathered his second kid. Not that he'll ever get to hold her."

"Dan was a friend, wasn't he?"

His nod was clipped—and not nearly as steady as his hand had been. "The best."

Her heart clenched as those still-reddened eyes began to shimmer. She stepped closer, reached out. But as the dampness welled up and threatened to spill, he jerked away and spun around. She followed him, reaching up to press her palm into the thick, quaking muscles of his shoulders.

"John?"

He shook his head. "Just—give me a sec." Dragging his air in deep, he lifted a hand to scrub his eyes. His breath shuddered out as he turned back. "Sorry. I'm fine. Today's...brought a bunch of stuff to a head."

LaCroix.

With everything that was going on in John's life, she wasn't sure how she could be so certain. But she was. The CID agent in her demanded she push it. The fellow soldier and woman in her cautioned patience, compassion. Especially the woman.

She listened to the latter.

An eternity seemed to pass as she stood there, silent. Waiting. And then agent, soldier and woman were rewarded with a soft, resigned sigh.

"It's Evan."

"Your houseguest?"

John nodded. "You were right about him."

"I was?"

"The night we met. You told me you were worried about the guy. You were right to be." John gripped the back of his neck as he blew out another sigh. "Ev's messed up. He has been for a while. And he's getting worse."

"How so?"

He lowered his hand. "He's been sounding off about the general."

"Ertonç?"

"Yeah. He headed up the campaign that killed Carys." John shook his head in disgust. *"Collateral damage.* Christ, I hate that phrase. Always have. Too goddamned innocuous for what it represents." His fingers came up again, this time to scrub at the grief that still tinged his eyes, but he couldn't quite seem to reach it all. He gave up, tucking his hand into the crook of his opposite arm. "Ertonç was a colonel before Operation Peace Spring. He made general after. Right after."

"Wow."

"Yup. Anyway, I thought—hoped—Evan had come to terms with it. But then he learned Ertonç was on his way here."

And that was her opening.

She reached out, laid her hand on John's forearm, atop the coarse, roping scar that fed up into that daunting biceps. "Why *is* he here?"

John shook his head. "Sorry. Can't say."

Damn. She smoothed the pads of her fingers down the mottled rope, drawing him back to his current, darker dilemma. "You're worried, aren't you? That Evan's going to do something stupid...or deadly."

Silence.

The air was thick with it. Tense.

Telling.

It was now or never. "Maybe..." She slid the tip of her tongue along her bottom lip. "Maybe you should...say something."

"To whom?"

"I don't know. His commanding officer? Yours? CID?"

"Can't." John shook his head, but he didn't step back. "I don't have proof. Just my gut and the drunken spewings of a fellow soldier still racked with grief. It's not enough to risk his career over. A damned stellar career."

"But what if your gut's right? The general's in town." Ertonç was being watched, yes. Protected. But LaCroix wasn't. And *he* was SF, with all the cold, deadly skills the specialty entailed. The ones he excelled at. "What if Evan's out there right now—"

"He's not."

"You can't be sure."

"I can. I am." A revealing flush tinged John's neck, highlighting the stark white of those twin overlapping scars that tangled down beneath the collar of his matching tee. "I'm having him watched."

Watched. "As in...guarded?"

"Yes." He did withdraw from her then. Physically and emotionally. Or perhaps he was simply withdrawing from himself and what he'd just admitted to doing to a fellow soldier —and friend. He took a step back and turned to the coffee table to retrieve the bottle of whiskey and its cap. "I needed some time to get my head on straight, to toast Stubbs and mourn him, so I asked a buddy to look out for Evan tonight. He'll give me a heads up when Ev heads home. If he heads home. Lately, Ev's been choosing that bar you and I met at over his bed."

Relief filtered in with the reassurance that LaCroix wasn't out there alone. And who better to guard the sergeant than one of his own?

Regan stepped up to the coffee table. To John.

He'd capped the bottle, but he was still staring at it as though mesmerized by the amber swirling within.

She reached down and retrieved the empty glass. "It's okay if you have another."

She hated herself for making the suggestion, especially having read the horrors in that BI of his. But if the man had more of that whiskey, she just might get more information. Enough to obtain a warrant to access that room down the hall and end this damned thing. Before LaCroix hit the town *unguarded*.

"No." John retrieved the tumbler from her hand and set it and the bottle on the table—firmly. "I was serious earlier; I have the one. Just the one. And *only* when I lose someone."

"Why?" But she knew. Though it hadn't been spelled out in that BI, it was in there. And it was right here. In that strained, distant stare. Along with all the things she was not supposed to know about this man—much less feel for him.

She almost wished he wouldn't answer.

But he did. "My dad." The ghosts haunting those dark gray eyes strengthened. Multiplied. Crowded out the hope. "I didn't tell you everything last night. Didn't want to scare you off. Hell, I've probably done that anyway."

"You haven't."

"Yeah?" He didn't even try to hide his doubt, much less the gnawing pain and anger. "Let's just say I watched the man crawl into too damned many bottles while I was growing up. And each time he'd beat the shit out of me before he crawled back out. It's why my mom took Beth when she split—and left me with the bastard. She was afraid I'd turn out just like him. Maybe I will. Could be I just haven't hit the right trigger. Yet."

He fell silent, waiting.

Accusing.

He expected her to leave him too. If not now, or later tonight —soon. That betraying pulse of his bellowed it. Dared her to *just go*. Like his mom and his sister. The friend he'd lost today. And all the other friends and fellow soldiers he'd lost as that bottle— and countless previous ones—had been drained, inch by agonizing inch. He was all but begging her to leave. Before it was too late.

For him.

She wasn't going anywhere.

She reached up and cupped his jaw, directly over that trio of shrapnel scars. She could feel his pulse thundering beneath her palm. He was livid.

But he didn't push her away.

"You're nothing like your dad."

"How would you know?"

"I just do." And not because she'd read his BI. Her hand slipped down to his shoulder. "My grandfather wasn't exactly gentle when he disciplined. He had this worn leather strap he liked to use when I failed to live up to his particular interpretation of the scriptures. My Sunday school teacher saw the welts and bruises once and called him out. But that just...

made it worse." Not that the man had really needed a reason to whale on her, though she hadn't understood that at the time. Her failings had simply been his excuse. A way to deal with the humiliation of his son-in-law's betrayal. And his daughter's subsequent suicide.

John's jaw shifted beneath her palm as he swallowed—hard. "Where the hell was your mother?"

"She...died a couple months after my dad." It was true. Mostly. That was what mattered—right?

"So, you grew up with a bastard too."

She shook her head.

"Don't tell me he died as well."

"Heart attack. I was nine." It was almost a relief by then. "I was too old for adoption." Too standoffish and stubborn. Too much baggage. Hers, her mom's. Her dad's. Hell, even her grandfather's. "I went in the system."

"Foster care?"

"Yeah."

"How many homes?"

"I don't know. I didn't keep track."

Liar.

He knew it too, because his fingers came up to soothe her cheek. To soothe *her.* Given the man's size, it was amazing how gentle he could be. But that ragged pulse was not. Her fingertips took on a life of their own, reaching up to mirror his touch as she traced a path through the evening stubble on his cheek.

The pulse picked up, thumping into her palm once more. This time for an entirely different reason.

He turned his face into her hand and kissed it. She opened her mouth, but before she could say anything, he'd pulled her close and was kissing her.

He didn't need to coax desire from her tonight. It was there, searing in with that first touch of his lips.

She felt those familiar, proprietary hands of his sliding in as well, then down to engulf her lower back and ass as he pulled her closer still. His tongue swept deep, fanning the flames between them for several long, increasingly torrid kisses—until the flames were raging. Part of her knew they were being fueled by the raw emotions they'd just shared; the rest of her didn't care.

Nor did he.

Because the fire was consuming them both.

Her clothes seemed to disintegrate from her body, along with his. Or maybe the fabric had been singed off. She couldn't be sure. All she knew for certain was that both of them were finally, blissfully, down to scarred, bunching muscle and sleek, sinuous flesh. His callused hands and hot, seeking mouth were everywhere now. It wasn't enough. She wanted more. Needed it.

She needed him.

She didn't protest as John lifted her up by her waist and encouraged her to wrap her legs around him as he moved to press her naked back into the wall, because his breathtakingly naked front was pressing firmly into her.

She did protest, however, when he broke his string of fiery kisses to rasp, *"Condom."*

"I'm safe."

She could feel the relief blistering through his massive form —and then he was suddenly, mercifully, blistering into her. Filling her.

Good Lord, *everything* about the man was huge.

He swallowed her gasp and groaned right back into her as he drove deeper, pushing the both of them higher, hotter, and harder—again and again—until their private scorching world imploded on a series of glorious, mind and body-racking shudders. His harsh breaths mingled with hers, filling the still-smoldering air as they drifted back down together.

Before she realized his intent, John had swung her back up into his arms, cradling her close as he turned to carry her out of the living room and down the hall.

"Where are we going?"

"To bed." For the first time that night, that disarming dent in his cheek cut in, along with his deeper, arrogantly satisfied grin. "As earth shattering as that was, it barely took the edge off. We're going to do that again. And, this time—" Both dent and arrogance dipped deeper. "I plan on taking my time."

SHE WAS TRAPPED.

Regan stared at the solid wall of muscle beneath her left cheek as one of those proprietary hands of John's shifted from the back of her shoulder. It slipped down past her waist, then hip, until it was cupping her entire ass as though it had every right. Which, given how they'd just spent the last three hours, it did.

What the *hell* had she done?

And how did she extricate herself from this king-sized bed without waking its king-sized owner who, even in his post-grief and endorphin-induced sleep, managed to keep her entire body fused to the length of his?

She refused to rush. It was barely eleven. She had time to figure out her plan of attack.

Make that retreat. A full-on, panic and guilt-driven retreat.

And then she heard it.

Her phone.

The ringtone was faint, but that trilling was definitely hers. This late, there were only a handful of callers who'd be trying to reach her. And only if it was critical that they do so. She had to get out of here to take that call.

In private.

She winced as the phone trilled again—and John's torso shifted. She was now trapped more firmly than before. A thick swath of her hair was caught beneath the man's mammoth shoulder. She tried lifting her head and gently tugging, but that caused his chest to move again. Worse, he'd roused enough to murmur that name she'd come to detest.

"Rachel."

She held her breath and waited for him to settle. He did—until the phone trilled once more, and he shifted once more. One way or another, the slumbering giant was going to rouse. With nothing left to lose, she slipped across the front of that hardened body, tugging her hair from beneath his shoulder as she stood.

He sighed...and drifted into a deeper sleep.

Determined to keep him there, she retrieved the comforter from where it had fallen to the floor and carefully settled it over his legs and torso to help replace the warmth he'd lost when she'd abandoned the bed, and him.

As for her, she was buck naked. Her clothes were still strewn across the floor of the living room with her phone. At the far end of the hall.

Was LaCroix home?

She actually prayed he wasn't.

Either way, her phone was still ringing. Gooseflesh born more of desperation than the surrounding cold rippled over her body as she crept out of the darkened bedroom and down the hardwood slats of the hall. By the time she'd located her phone in the dim light of the single table lamp—beneath John's underwear—it had ceased ringing. She scooped the phone up regardless, along with her own underclothes, sweatshirt, jeans, shoes and leather bag, and headed into the darkened kitchen, once again praying she wouldn't run into LaCroix.

The room was empty. A quick glance out the window beside

the back door revealed two cars in the drive, the Tiguan and John's Wrangler. The sergeant was still barhopping with John's buddy then.

Thank God.

She turned away from the window, set her bag on the cooking island and began donning her clothes as rapidly as they'd been removed. Safely dressed, she retrieved her phone to check the caller ID.

Jelly. He'd left an unforgivably pithy text in lieu of voicemail. *Call me!!!*

She pushed back at the panic as she stepped into her running shoes. He could be letting her know Brooks had caved, that she was cleared to bring John in on the case.

Though with all that had happened here tonight—in the living room and in that bed down the hall—the possibility of finally coming clean didn't enthuse her nearly as much as it would've earlier in the day. Once John learned the truth, what were the odds he'd believe she hadn't slept with him to make her case? That she'd been as caught up in what'd been happening between them as he?

She tied her shoelaces and faced the kitchen's archway to keep watch for John as she dialed her fellow agent's number.

He picked up on the first ring.

"*What's up, Jelly?*"

"Rae? I can barely hear you. Is everything okay? Can you talk?"

She raised her voice, but not by much. "Yeah. The captain's... in another room." And she'd like to keep him there for as long as possible—asleep. "What happened?"

"We got a problem."

They were just piling up tonight, weren't they? "Explain."

"You asked me to dig deep into the doc."

Damn. "What popped?"

"Not sure yet, but the issue's not with him. It's the wife. She goes by the name of—" She heard papers rustling. "—Inci Karmandi."

"Goes by?" Dread trickled in at the phrasing.

"That's the problem. At first glance, Inci looks clean. Devoted doctor's wife, stay-at-home mom of a four-year-old boy and a bouncing baby girl. Birth certificates for the kids check out, as does the marriage license for her and the doc. But when I went back further, I found something odd. The trail goes cold. I found a current UK passport and a birth certificate for one Inci Yilmaz, but nothing in between. It's like she doesn't exist for those nineteen intervening years."

Nineteen? The number rattled deep within Regan's brain.

She dropped her gaze to the stainless-steel, motion-activated trash can tucked in the corner near the doorway. A small, yellow sticky note clung near the base of the can. "Inci's British?"

"According to those two records. The *only* two I found. Anywhere. I can't even get my hands on her visa application for the move to Germany."

That was seriously troubling. So was that number. Nineteen.

Damn, it—why?

The number locked into place. *"Shit."*

"What?"

"Check the date on the license. How long have Inci and the doc been married?"

"Just a sec."

Regan stared at that stray sticky as the sound of another round of paper rustling filtered through the connection. Reaching down, she snagged the square, along with the tiny wad of paper in the corner behind it. She could hear Jelly mumbling through the math as she straightened.

"Seven years."

Seven? Regan mashed the wad into the sticky, earning a

paper cut as the implications burned in. Seven years ago, John was in the middle of his first tour as an SF officer in Afghanistan, just outside Kabul. She was now all but certain she knew what he'd done to earn Ertonç's trust, as well as Ertonç's intercession with that Afghan warlord—and it was one hell of a favor. The kind that would put a then-colonel and now-general in John's debt for life. But to prove it, she'd need evidence. "Do you have a photo of Inci handy?"

"Just the one in the passport. And since she was nineteen at the time, it's a few years old. She's also wearing a headscarf, but—"

"Text it to me."

Regan stared at the yellow sticky as she waited. A drop of blood from the cut between her index finger and thumb had stained the edge scarlet. She flipped the sticky over and stared at the scrawl on the front. It was an address, located in the middle of the next town over. But the handwriting wasn't spiked like John's. Instead, the rounded numbers and letters resembled the samples Jelly had obtained of LaCroix's.

Was it his?

She tucked the sticky and wad of paper in the front pocket of her jeans as her text app pinged. She enlarged the enclosed photo—and cursed.

"Prez?"

She sealed the phone to her ear. "Sorry. Everything fine." But it wasn't. Headscarf or not, "I know who that is." She'd seen the same woman—then a fourteen-year-old girl—in a family photo with her still-living mother, two older brothers and father hours earlier while she'd been holed up in her room at the Lodge, reviewing everything she had that was remotely related to this case. "That's Saniye Ertonç—the general's daughter."

"The one that drowned?"

"Yup." Only she hadn't. Somehow, seven years ago, John had

discovered that Saniye was in love with a Christian Kurd and had faked her death for then-Colonel Ertonç.

Damned if the body language she'd observed these past few days didn't finally make sense—all of it. John and the general on the stage; John and the doc at the hospital. Including the general's preoccupation at the window in the conference room prior to the interview he'd granted her.

Ertonç had been oblivious to both her and the captain that morning. But not the scene outside. The soldier and his son. Only it wasn't the soldier who'd mesmerized Ertonç, so much as the boy and boy's indulgent, watching *mother.*

Seven years ago, while attending university in England, Saniye had fallen in love with the cousin of her father's enemy. Ertonç had been livid. But she was family; Ertonç wanted his daughter alive—but out of his life. And now that she was the only family member of his left alive, he wanted her back in.

Except, given the body language between John and Saniye's husband in that hospital, the woman didn't want back in.

John was involved in a classified, backchannel negotiation all right. Just not the one she'd assumed.

She'd bet her Rachel Pace cover identity that John had the Army's full support with his negotiations too. Because if it had been valuable to have a Turkish colonel indebted to Special Forces and the Army in Afghanistan, imagine the possibilities in having a Turkish brigadier general beholden to them now.

She was fairly certain she understood the timing too. Namely, why Ertonç had carefully arranged for his official military-to-military visit for five weeks hence, only to arrive earlier this week, on his own dime.

Regan craned her neck, peering out from the kitchen's archway into the dimly lit living room and down the darkened hall.

Both were quiet. Empty.

John was still fast asleep.

Even Brooks would agree that she not only had enough to prove John was in the clear, but also to wake him and confess all before asking him to access that guest room. And she would. Soon. But she wasn't looking forward to it. Not after what they'd done. What John was bound to assume about the case —and her.

"Jelly, you mentioned two kids. A boy and a baby girl. How old's the baby?"

"That I know without checking. She was born six days ago. In the same hospital you visited this morning. Not sure if it matters, but she was early. By over a month. Apparently, there was some kind of placental separation issue. Required an emergency cesarean. In fact, they had to call an ambulance out in the middle of the night to Vilseck. If the doc hadn't realized what was happening, Inci—or Saniye—could've died. Got that from the obstetrics nurse who—"

"Vilseck?" *Christ.* That was the town on the sticky. "I found a note hung up on the trash. It's in LaCroix's handwriting." It had to be his. She yanked the sticky from her pocket. "Do you have the address for the doc and his wife?"

"Yeah. It's—"

She rattled off the information along with Jelly. It matched. Somehow, the sergeant had not only figured out that Saniye Ertonç was still alive, but that she'd become Inci Karmandi. And he knew where she and her husband lived.

"Rae, we gotta get a tail on LaCroix—now."

"I know." Brooks would finally approve it, too. In a heartbeat. Because while Mira and the rest of that PSU detail were ensuring Ertonç's safety, no one was looking out for the general's daughter and her family. "Call Brooks. Let him know that LaCroix is out and about tonight, but he's not alone. The captain was worried about him so he tasked a buddy with babysitting.

They're barhopping—try the one we used for the initial honeytrap. I want that tail nailed to his ass before he returns home." She turned to the island to grab her bag. "I'm headed to the office. I'll see you in a few."

She hung up and shoved the phone into her pocket. But as she reached for her bag, she remembered the wad of paper.

If the sticky had fallen from LaCroix's hand while he'd been dumping his guest room trash...was the wad his too?

She pulled it out and returned to the archway to use the light bleeding in from the living room lamp as she unraveled the paper.

It was a receipt from a local florist.

Regan stiffened as she spotted the itemized tally for an oversized teddy bear, a roll of gift wrap and a trio of eleven-inch latex balloons. Pink.

What better way to disguise a bomb?

Even more chilling, she and Jelly had purchased a dozen latex balloons several months back to celebrate a fellow agent's promotion, only to become annoyed when they'd lost their collective *oomph* and sunk to the floor by the following night. According to the receipt, these balloons had been filled with helium that morning—when John had been at the hospital with her.

Not only was the receipt LaCroix's, the clock on the sergeant's carefully crafted revenge was already counting down.

Damn it, she had *time*. LaCroix was being watched. If he was about to make his move, she'd know. Because John would know.

The knowledge kept the bulk of her panic at bay—until a phone rang. The sound wasn't coming from her back pocket. It was coming from the crumpled jeans less than a yard from her shoes.

John's jeans.

It rang again, the deep trill reverberating straight through her, across the living room and down into John's bedroom at the far end of the hall. She could hear him rising up from the bed and moving off. His door opening.

"Rachel?"

Shit. She didn't have time to answer, much less explain. Not if that call was about LaCroix.

Not if she hoped to save Saniye's life.

Regan shoved the receipt in her pocket and spun around, grabbing her bag and her keys on her way to the back door of the kitchen. She cleared the house and raced across the darkened drive to vault into the Tiguan. Within seconds, she'd fired up the engine and was using the car's hands-free feature to dial Jelly as she backed the car into the street and spun it around toward Vilseck.

Three agonizing rings in, Jelly picked up. "Just got off the phone with Brooks. He says—"

"Call him back! Have him dispatch SWAT and a bomb disposal team to the Karmandi home! I'm on my way there— LaCroix is executing his attack *now.*"

If he hadn't already.

8

Regan reached the heart of Vilseck in record time.

Unfortunately, LaCroix had arrived first.

Though that dark, sweater-clad back was roughly sixty yards away and on the opposite side of the divided, mostly residential street, it was him. Who else would be carrying a three-foot box covered in pastel-pink wrapping paper with a trio of matching latex balloons and a froth of ribbons floating behind him shortly before midnight?

Make that forty yards from her now—and twenty from the door of that ice-blue, two-story Bavarian home.

The Karmandi home.

A fresh wave of adrenaline coursed through her veins as she hit the brakes and swerved to the right, pulling the Tiguan off the paved road and onto the flanking cobblestone walk. She killed the engine and grabbed her bag, slipping her fingers into the hidden compartment within.

Seconds later, she and her 9mm Sig Sauer were bailing out of the VW and heading across the blessedly otherwise deserted road. By the time she'd reached the grassy divider, LaCroix was less than five yards from the white-washed door of the Bavarian stucco. A single light burned from within. She could only pray that whoever'd left it lit had long since fallen asleep.

"US Army CID! Stop right there, Sergeant. Gently lower the package to the ground, then turn around—slowly."

The man stopped. But he didn't lower the box, much less turn. Though his head did shift far enough to the left to catch their reflections in the windows of the car parked in front of the Karmandi home.

"Now, Sergeant."

"Evening, Rachel. Well, this makes sense now, doesn't it? Though, if you're CID, I seriously doubt that's your name. How about you introduce—"

The piercing wail of a German police car bearing down on their location drowned out the rest. Moments later, several more joined in, obliterating the surreal calm of the darkened street.

The cavalry had arrived.

One by one, the sirens cut out as the vehicles closed in.

It was too late. Another light had fired up inside the Karmandi home, then another, as half a dozen silent, pulsing red, white and blue strobes pulled up on both sides of Regan and the primary focus of her attention.

The white-washed door opened. A curious Olan Karmandi stood inside its frame, peering out—with his swaddled, days-old daughter in his arms.

"Go back inside, doctor! Don't—"

"Luftballons, Papa!"

Shit. Karmandi's pajama-clad son had spotted the giant gift-wrapped box and darted out past the hem of his father's robe.

"Sener, Halt!"

The four-year-old boy froze five feet from the sergeant and his deceptively cheery burden. Tears welled up, splashing down onto pale, chubby cheeks as the boy stared at the 9mm in her hands.

The one sighted in on the back of LaCroix's cropped, dark-blond curls.

Regan forced herself to remain where she was, even as the sergeant took a step away from her and toward the now openly sobbing child.

"Evan, don't do this."

He stopped. "Evan?" He shook his head as he *tsked* softly. Pointedly. "I'm afraid we don't know each other that well, do we —*Rachel?*"

"Regan. Special Agent Regan Chase."

He nodded, but still didn't turn. Much less lower that damned box. He did, however, remain where he was. "Nice to meet you, Regan."

"Let the boy go back inside, Evan."

"He can go as far as his dad. But if he takes one step further—"

"He won't!" shouted Karmandi. "You have my word." Though the doc had addressed LaCroix, he was alternating that tortured stare of his between her and his son. Karmandi might not understand what was going on, but he was smart enough to know that an armed special agent wouldn't be all but on his doorstep, trying to talk a man with a package out of moving closer unless it was serious.

Deadly serious.

"*Sener, Komm!*"

The boy spun around and ran to his father.

The doc grabbed the collar of Sener's green footie pjs and held on for all he was worth before the kid could dart past. "Please, let me take the children to my wife. I will return shortly —I swear."

"But it's your wife I want."

Confusion clouded into Karmandi's bloodless features, before coalescing into full-blown terror as the explanation punched in. Given the two US soldiers at odds in front of him—and who else was in town—there was only one possibility. Ertonç.

Regan risked a step forward, then another.

"I can hear you creeping, Agent Chase."

She froze. And adjusted the aim on her 9mm until it was dead center on the base of those closely-cropped curls. "I'm armed, Evan."

"Figured as much."

She winced at the whisper of Jelly's nearly imperceptible tread closing in as he took up a supporting position on her right.

"Tell that lumbering ox he'd better stand fast too."

Regan caught Jelly's terse, freckled nod in her periphery, even as she focused on the soldier in front of her. "Put the box down, Evan. You don't want to do this."

"Oh, I do. And you know why, don't you? And why it has to be her?"

"I know." The sergeant's logic in choosing the aimpoint for his revenge was chilling, but brilliant. Why murder the man responsible for killing the woman he loved, when LaCroix could let Ertonç live with the horrific knowledge, day in and day out, that the fallout from his decisions in Syria had caused LaCroix to slaughter the only woman left that Ertonç loved...and quite possibly her entire family? Especially since the damage to NATO would be the same. "Now, put the box down."

"Or what?"

"I'll shoot."

"In front of the kid?"

"If I must." And she would. Because he was not getting any closer to that door with those two rigid bodies and that tiny, bundled form. "But it wouldn't be in front of him, would it?" Karmandi had shifted his grip, using the collar of those green pj's to force his son's face behind his quivering, robe-clad thigh.

All Sener could see was the far wall of the paneled foyer.

As for Karmandi, he might be a physician, but she didn't think he'd suffer too many nightmares over the outcome she threatened. At least not regretful ones. Not with his children's lives at stake.

LaCroix left those realities unaddressed. Nor did he order a halt to the fresh wave of muted footfalls along the pavement behind her and Jelly. She flicked a glance toward the parked car's windows and caught the reflected mixed marriage of German and US Army police moving into position amid the pulsing lights.

"If you shoot, I'll drop the box. I put in a mercury switch. It's my specialty. If you've done your research—and given how you look, I know you have—you know I'm telling the truth. One slight tip and—*boom*. The box explodes and we all die. You, me, the doc and those two kids, along with the rest of that herd of uniformed oxen behind us. Of course, I could be lying. But are you willing to take the chance?"

He was right about the mercury switch. He did have a thing for them. But it was a bluff. One she might've fallen for if she hadn't spotted the slender tag nestled amid that froth of pink ribbon hanging down from those balloons. If he'd attached that tag to the package, she'd have never seen it.

Not from this angle.

She took a step forward. "No."

"No, you didn't do your due diligence? Or, no, you don't care if we all die?"

"No, it won't explode." She took another step, then another. And another. One final step, and she had the 9mm's muzzle pressing into that blond stubble at the base of his skull. She had to give LaCroix credit. He didn't flinch.

"How can you be so sure?"

"The tag."

He actually glanced up. "What about it?"

"It's made out to Saniye."

"So?"

"Most people who wrap up a giant bear will address the tag to the baby." Especially if they've taken the time to toss in all that pink. "You didn't even add Olan's name. You addressed it to Saniye—and only Saniye—because you wanted her to open it." Hell, he *needed* her to. The sergeant also needed Ertonç to know he knew exactly who he'd targeted. So much so, he'd inked Saniye's birth name onto an oversized tag and hung it from the base of the balloons to increase the odds that at least part of her name would survive the explosion. "That bomb's rigged to go off the moment the general's sole remaining child sees that tag, assumes it's a gift from her father, and opens the box that came with those balloons. Not before. Not after. *Now put it down.*"

The moment LaCroix bent his knees to comply, Jelly moved in, along with half a dozen German and US Army police. Not only were the latter unnecessary, the cuffing was downright anticlimactic. The sergeant just stood there while Jelly hooked him up. Silent, patient. Resigned.

Until Jelly spun the man around.

LaCroix stared at her then, studying her at length for the first time since she'd planted herself on that barstool days earlier. He actually smiled, chipmunk cheeks on full display. "CID, huh? Not quite as fresh from the deli as John Boy thinks, eh? He's gonna be pissed."

She reached for LaCroix's arm, but Jelly shook his head. "I'll take it from here. The locals are multiplying. Reporters and cameras won't be far behind. You'd best leave now, Prez, before your cover's blown far and wide."

As much as she wanted to personally toss LaCroix's handcuffed hide into the back of a patrol vehicle, Jelly was right.

Regan nodded her thanks.

As she turned to depart, LaCroix let out a chuckle. "That's not her only problem. John Boy's got zero tolerance for liars. And when he finds out he fucked one?" The sergeant's whistle was as low and taunting as that laugh had been. "Pissed won't begin to cover it."

"I—"

"Don't bother denying it. The captain was so into you, he forgot to close the blinds. Saw it all, Chief. Right up to the moment he scooped you up and sprinted down the hall for seconds. Now, don't get me wrong. I'm glad he got some. It's been a while. And I hope you enjoyed it too, because that man is never, *ever* gonna forgive you."

She turned her back on LaCroix's latest laugh—and the awkward pity in Jelly's carefully averted stare—and headed for her car.

She had no idea if any of the other soldiers or German police had heard, let alone understood. Nor did she want to know.

Hell, she couldn't even drive back to John's house. Even if she had been eager to confess all, apologies and explanations would have to wait. She had a suspect to process. Paperwork to file, and a case to wrap up.

By the time Regan tossed her 9mm into the Tiguan and crawled in after, she could see Karmandi handing off the baby to his wife amid the still-flashing strobes across the street. The doc removed his housecoat next, revealing a set of gray sweats. He passed the robe off too—this time to a waiting policeman—then reached out to smooth a strand of dark, sleep-mussed hair behind his wife's ear. He leaned close to give her a kiss before turning to follow a camouflaged soldier to a desert-sand truck. Within minutes, he'd be at the station, providing his statement.

His father-in-law wouldn't be far behind.

Hell, Ertonç might already be there. She'd know soon enough.

With the keys still in the Tiguan's ignition, Regan fired it up and executed a tight u-turn off the cobbled walkway and onto the now blocked-off road that led to Hohenfels. She could feel the effects of the sustained rush as the adrenaline began to ebb from her blood. She needed to get back on post and into her office at CID, and soon—before the brunt of the withdrawal hit.

She made it in the nick of time, though not quite as far as she'd hoped. She was pulling into the parking lot and past yet another cluster of desert-sand trucks and Humvees when the tremors began.

As she killed the VW's engine, she spotted Mira's profile just before the NCIS agent turned into the building, along with another soldier from the protective detail. Ertonç had arrived, then. She needed to get in there too. Take the general's statement personally. She owed Ertonç that much.

Hell, she owed John.

Unfortunately, she couldn't risk climbing out of the car. Not with the shakes hitting so hard her teeth had begun to chatter. She lowered her forehead and pressed it into the steering wheel as she willed them to cease.

They grew worse.

What if she'd been wrong about that gift tag? Where would Karmandi, his son and that days-old bundle be then?

Damn it, she *hadn't* been wrong. The Karmandis were okay.

All of them.

NATO was okay, too. For now.

She closed her eyes and dragged her breath in, then slowly pushed it out. Over and over, until the chattering and trembling eased.

Only then did she peel her forehead from the steering wheel. She caught a glimpse of her face in the rearview mirror and blanched.

She still had bedhead from, well, bed.

She grabbed her leather bag from the passenger seat and located a hairband from within. She scraped the tangled strands up into an oversized, makeshift bun and used the thick band to secure it. Plumbing the depths of the bag once more, she retrieved the 9mm's holster and her CID badge, along with two evidence bags.

The sticky note and florist receipt from John's kitchen went into the latter, separately.

It was time.

Hooking her 9mm and gold shield to the waistband of her jeans, she purged the remainder of her doubts as she grabbed the evidence bags and bailed out of the car.

Her phone pinged as she entered the building.

The text was from Mira, letting her know she was at the station, along with the general. But there was another notification on the screen too. An older one that'd come in during that frantic drive to Vilseck. This one was from John.

everything ok? call me

"Agent Chase?"

Regan flinched. She clicked off her phone and shoved it in her back pocket as she turned toward the young, black MP headed up the hall. "Yes, Corporal?"

"The witness parade's begun, and it's already gettin' hairy. Agent Jellin's not back yet. I texted Capt'n Brooks, but he must still be in with the post commander, because he hasn't answered neither. Sergeant Hernandez didn't want him waitin' any longer so he went in, but we're not sure how much to say."

No surprise there. Turkish or not, a general was still a general. No wonder Hernandez was stressed. "I'll handle it. Which room?"

The corporal tipped his buzz cut to the door slightly behind him and off his right. "Should I bring coffee?"

With the adrenaline purged from her blood, she'd have

crawled back to Hohenfels on her hands and knees to accept it. Unfortunately, her pending caffeinated status depended on the general's wishes, not hers.

"I'll let you know." She stepped past the MP and pushed through the door to the interview room. "Sorry to keep you waiting, sir. Captain Brooks is—"

The rest jammed up at the middle of her throat as she spotted the massive, tee shirt-clad back seated across the table from Hernandez. The titanic torso and solid shoulders within did not belong to Ertonç.

They belonged to John.

For some reason, he was here at the station, turning to stare at her, as utterly stunned as she. Scratch that; he was definitely more stunned. Until he stood and swung his entire body around to take hers in. She watched as suspicion crashed through the confusion, only to give way to damning comprehension—and the ice-cold anger she'd seen in this man once before. In his drive two nights ago when LaCroix had interrupted that goodnight kiss with his crude crack. And now, that anger was focused on her.

She stood there and accepted it. Absorbed it.

What choice did she have?

Despite the dyed hair and green-tinted contacts she'd yet to remove, she'd thoroughly shed Rachel Pace along with her clothes onto this man's living room floor five hours earlier. She hadn't donned the woman since. Not that John would believe her. Not with that icy stare of his growing icier by the second as he took in the mist-green wrinkled sweatshirt and jeans he'd personally stripped from her limbs...along with the gold shield now firmly attached to her waist.

It was the shield that condemned her. That, and the compact, black Sig Sauer P228 at her hip. Most US Army officers carried the larger, desert-tan P320.

But then, she wasn't even a commissioned officer, was she?

Sergeant Hernandez chose that moment to remember his manners. The stocky MP came to his feet. "Sir, this is Chief Warrant Officer Two Regan Chase, CID. Special Agent Chase has been running the LaCroix investigation."

The confirmation caused a flare in that carefully banked fury, searing off the ice. Pure, molten steel roiled beneath. John felt used. It was in every inch of those rigidly clenched muscles beneath the wrinkled tee and jeans that he, too, had recently picked up off the floor of his living room.

Along with the rest.

The condemnation and worse. The anger and suspicion she could've handled. Even that palpable regret. But the betrayal and the hurt?

Those cut straight through her.

John was wrong. He hadn't had sex with some faux cover identity. He'd had it with *her*. But she didn't have a cherub's chance in hell of convincing him of that now. Not with Hernandez three feet away, picking up on all those simmering vibes. Not to mention the digital voice recorder on the table. The one that was still actively listening in, sucking up for posterity every single word that'd been said in here before she'd arrived— and was yet to be said.

Once they were alone.

She left the door open, nodding to the MP as she stepped all the way into the room. "I've got this, Sergeant."

Curiosity warred with duty.

Fortunately, duty conquered quickly, and with a brisk nod. "Of course, Chief. For what it's worth, we'd barely gotten started. Captain Garrison came in on his own to make an unsolicited statement regarding Sergeant LaCroix. He had some concerns about the man, but hasn't had a chance to relay the specifics. I did inform him the sergeant was recently arrested while trying to place a bomb outside a civilian house in Vilseck. The captain knows the intended victims."

John had come in on his own? What on earth had he learned about LaCroix in the last hour? It must have been significant to force a one-eighty shift regarding his views on reporting the man.

She offered the MP an equally brisk nod. "Thank you, Sergeant. Please let Special Agent Ellis know I've arrived and that I'll speak with her and the general soon."

"Yes, Chief." The MP took a moment to face the voice recorder, verbally turning over the interview to her before he stepped away to depart the room.

Regan waited for the door to close before she risked approaching the abandoned chair. Unfortunately, John still loomed over the opposing side of the table, stiff and silent as he watched her unhook her shield from her waist. She set it down next to the recorder, along with the evidence bags containing the sticky note and florist receipt.

She could feel John studying her every motion, waiting for her to finish, to look up. Daring her.

She did.

"CID." Soft, damning. The rest was in his eyes. Why?

How?

She forced a shrug as she commandeered the MP's chair. "People see what they want to see. What they expect." Given where they were—and that dutifully vigilant recorder—it was all she could offer. She could only pray he'd be willing to listen to the rest once this was done.

Though, given the thunderous pace of that telltale pulse, she doubted it.

She tipped her head toward the empty chair beside him.

John ignored it for several long moments, then finally gathered his lingering anger and resentment and pulled them in deep. Cold acceptance slid into place as he nodded curtly and sat. "I guess they do."

Regan entered her true name, rank and the relative case stats into the recorder, only to find that frosted stare still locked on her as she finished. All morning, she'd wondered what it would cost her to return to John's home. What it would cost him. And would he ever be able to forgive her when it was over?

She had her answer.

So be it.

She dove in. "So, Captain, you're here on your own. I confess, I'm surprised. When we spoke earlier this evening, you mentioned your worries regarding Sergeant First Class Evan LaCroix and his outrage with Brigadier General Ertonç, as well as your fears that the sergeant might be in danger of spiraling out of control. But you didn't have proof that LaCroix had anything specific planned, much less that he was about to follow through. I assume something changed?"

That pulse picked up. But he nodded calmly. Too calmly, given everything that was still unsaid. "Correct. As I also mentioned earlier, I asked a fellow officer to watch out for the sergeant tonight. After you...*left*...I received a call from Captain Trussell. LaCroix had given him the slip a couple hours earlier."

No surprise there. Not after the sergeant's parting shot following his arrest. Still, "Hours? And Trussell was just calling?"

Fire raged beneath the ice. It was quickly controlled and re-banked. "No. That was his fourth call. I'd left my phone in another room while I...slept. Given my concern for the sergeant, Truss was about to head over to see if something had happened, but he'd decided to try once more."

"I see. And then?"

"I hung up. I was worried about another...friend. So, I texted *her*—"

Shit.

"—and that's when I noticed a text I'd missed. It was from Evan. I thought—" He broke off, shook his head as if still unnerved by the text's contents. "I thought it was a suicide note."

Christ. "May I see it?"

The molten gray churned anew, but he nodded. John retrieved his phone from his back pocket and opened his text app, then slid it across the table.

You're right, man—I am fucked up. I made my decision. Thanks for hanging in as long as you did. Don't blame yourself.

It did sound as though LaCroix had planned on ending things. And he had—just not his own life. At least, not until he'd taken Saniye's.

She took a screen shot of the text and forwarded it to her own phone, then opened John's conversation stream with her to ensure it had sent.

In retrospect, it might not have been the best decision.

She'd have gotten a copy of the same information by accessing LaCroix's cellular account once the warrants came through. And she wouldn't have sent John's phone scooting back across the table with his last text to her now open on the screen.

everything ok?

Not by a long shot. And it was getting longer.

She could feel John recalling every moment they'd spent together as he looked up from that text, replaying every confidence and confession he'd offered her in light of what he now knew about her. And every confidence and confession she'd supposedly gifted him. She wasn't coming off well. Worse, she deserved it.

She'd become her dad after all.

At least in this man's eyes.

The case, damn it. Focus on the case. "The sergeant mentions a decision. To what was he referring?"

"We had an argument. The night you came over for dinner.

After you left, I told him what I thought was the truth." John's inflection on that last left no doubt he now knew otherwise. Unfortunately, inflection wouldn't stand up in court.

"The truth?"

"That some SF sergeant said you were a ringer for Carys. I told him I realized that's why his mood had gone to hell, but—painful reminder or not—like his former housemate, I'd had it with his attitude and his digs. I assured him the rest of the Army wouldn't be far behind. I told him he had two choices: get his shit together, or get the fuck out. And I didn't just mean my house. I figured he'd sent that text to let me know he'd chosen the latter, just not the way I'd assumed. But as I said, I didn't know that when I first saw his text."

"How did you discover his plans?" Because he must have. Why else had John shown up here?

"I'd called him back, but it went to voicemail. So, I sent a text. Hell, I probably sent a dozen in half as many minutes—all unanswered. So, I went to his room." He shrugged as though he was still embarrassed he'd invaded the man's privacy. "I was desperate. I found his computer, got lucky when I typed in Carys' name at the password prompt. But then I became even more worried when I realized he'd cleaned everything out. Emails, texts, browser history, bookmarks—they were all missing. I'm not even sure why I checked his maps app. Part of me hoped I might be able to figure out where he'd gone to off himself. Anyway, that's when I spotted it. And then I knew."

"It?" She knew too, but she needed *it* spelled out for the recorder.

"The Karmandi address."

"He wasn't supposed to have it, was he?"

"No one was. Not even the general. And that was Ertonç's decision, not mine."

"I don't understand."

John sighed. "You'd have to go back a few years, and over a subcontinent if you want to do that."

"You're referring to what you did for then-Colonel Ertonç in Kabul."

He captured her stare for a moment and held it. Nodded. "I guess you figured that out too."

"I think so. I know about Dr. Karmandi's cousin Royar and Royar's connection to the PKK and the car bombing that killed the general's sons in Inçirlik last year. Learning of Ertonç's extremely personal hatred for Kurds years before the bombing, along with a few other facts, allowed me to extrapolate the rest —eventually. I assume Saniye and Dr. Karmandi met while she was still in England, since that's where she supposedly died."

John nodded. "Saniye was a student; Olan was already a physician. Both were volunteering at a clinic for immigrants. I happened to be with her father when he found out she was dating a Kurd. And, yes, that's when and why his hatred turned personal—but it grew worse. Ertonç tracked me down the following week. Saniye had called to tell him she and Olan were marrying and moving to Germany, with or without his blessing. He was enraged. But he was also terrified she'd be killed as a message to him, either by someone in the PKK or another Turk who wanted to make an example of her. I offered to contact a buddy with the CIA to make her disappear safely. Ertonç wanted me to go further. He wanted her dead to the world—and he didn't want the CIA involved. He didn't trust them. Only a select few, very hefty links up my chain of command were allowed to know, and even they weren't to be privy to her new identity. The links agreed, so I got to work."

"You faked her drowning."

He shrugged. "It seemed the easiest option. Everyone knew she had asthma and there was no need to produce a body since it had supposedly been swept out to sea. Everything was fine until her brothers were murdered in retaliation for Ertonç's role in Operation Peace Spring. Saniye was devastated—but Olan was enraged. With Royar. He called Ertonç to apologize on behalf of all Kurds. Ertonç hung up on him. But as the general's grief began to ease, he realized he had only one male blood relative left in the world. His grandson. The boy was half-Kurdish. But if his son-in-law could humble himself when he'd known he'd be cut off, maybe some Kurds were different. And Ertonç began to believe that maybe, just maybe, it was up to him to help his people accept that. So Ertonç contacted me and asked me to broker a meeting. As I'm sure you figured out, I bought that burner to keep their conversations off the Turkish government's radar. When I delivered it, Olan was wary, but ultimately willing; Saniye wasn't. She wouldn't speak to him, even after he showed up here following her emergency delivery."

"That was what that phone exchange I noted during the general's interview was about, wasn't it?"

"Yes."

No wonder Ertonç had been unnerved. He'd been soundly rejected by his sole surviving child. "And when I saw you and Dr. Karmandi at the hospital arguing, that was you trying to convince him to persuade his wife to reconsider."

John nodded. "I suggested a formal visit to his hospital. To the public and press—since Germany has a substantial Kurdish population—it would look like a Turkish general making nice with a few Kurdish doctors and patients, including Saniye's husband. While Saniye would see her father breaking through his bigotry and publicly accepting her husband and the father of her children. Olan agreed that if Ertonç was genuinely respectful to everyone during the visit, he'd convince her to meet with her father. Guess we won't need to resort to that now. Not after everything that's happened tonight."

It was true. Father and daughter would now meet. At the sergeant's court-martial if not elsewhere.

The irony of it. LaCroix would be pissed to discover he was the instrument which had brought it about. If Saniye and her father did manage to heal the familial breach, it would be because of him.

As for the breach that had formed between herself and the man sitting across the table from her, that one was growing wider by the second. With each new revelation—hers and his—John's body language grew colder, more remote. Even now, she could feel him pulling away from her emotionally as well.

She deserved it.

But it still hurt.

He jerked his chin toward the evidence bags she'd laid on the table. The one with the yellow sticky was on top. He knew as well as she did whose handwriting was on it. "How'd you get that?"

"I found it in your kitchen, hung up on the outside of your trash."

His stare found hers once more. The molten gray within had coalesced and forged into an unforgiving iron. "Tonight?"

"Yes."

"So, I did hear you sneaking out the back door."

She was fairly certain he noticed the flush staining the base of her neck as she nodded—because she could definitely feel it.

She shifted her gaze until it settled pointedly on the recorder, painfully aware it was still soaking up every sound in the room. Hell, both he and that microphone had to be hearing the pounding in her chest. Lord knew she could.

To her relief, John took the hint and sighed. "Like I said, Evan wasn't supposed to have that address. Not only was it classified, it was stored in just two places. The first was my head. The second was in a file on an encrypted hard drive, to be accessed if need be and *only* if something had happened to me. That encrypted drive is currently plugged into my computer...at work."

Meaning John wasn't the only one who'd accessed a laptop that wasn't his. But he'd been motivated by the life of a fellow soldier.

LaCroix had not.

Worse, the sergeant had done more than violate a friend's trust. He'd violated the US Army's. The former was inexcusable. The latter, a crime punishable by the UCMJ. It was also enough to send LaCroix to a cell at Fort Leavenworth, even without tonight's events in Vilseck added on.

"And then you headed here."

"Correct. Since it contained proof, I brought his laptop with me. Your sergeant signed it into evidence before we came in here. I was worried for an entirely new reason. I knew if Evan was willing to break into my classified files, he was willing to go all the way. And I knew where he was eventually headed." He flicked his stare toward the sticky. "Apparently, you'd figured it out first. But how the hell did you know he was going to act tonight?"

She reached out to lift the uppermost evidence bag from the table, revealing the one beneath. "It's a receipt from a German florist. According to the timestamp, LaCroix purchased an oversized teddy bear, wrapping paper and a trio of pink latex balloons while you and I were at the hospital yesterday morning. The latter were filled with helium while he waited."

"So, the countdown had begun, and you knew it."

She nodded.

"And that receipt. Was it also in my trash?"

Regan thought about clarifying its precise location, but she didn't. She knew full well that if the receipt had been buried deep inside the can instead of wadded up on the floor—and she'd known—she'd have dug through to retrieve it and anything else that had the potential to help her solve her case. Because lives had been at stake.

The Karmandis were worth it. Sener and his newborn sister were worth it.

But where had their need for safety left her?

"Guess Ev cleaned out more than his laptop history today. Quite the houseguest."

That he was. Somehow, John's guest had managed to clean them out too.

Wrong. She'd accomplished that all by herself, hadn't she?

The thick, roping scar feeding up from John's wrist all the way into his biceps turned stark white as he folded his arms. He leaned back in his chair to study her. "There was no article on Ertonç, was there?"

"No." It wasn't as though she could splice Rachel Pace into a byline, let alone Regan Chase. "But I did give Terry the notes I took during the interview you arranged. He's hoping to use them himself. When this is over."

"Terry." It was a statement, not a question. And not about the man, but his rank. Though Terry was also a captain, she hadn't addressed him as such—as she'd done with John. Right up to that kiss in his driveway. "So, you and *Terry*—"

"He's a friend."

"One you've used to cover your lies before? In your...work."

"I'm sorry, I can't—"

"Right."

Irony bit in again as those shadows returned. Swimming among them were all the questions John now had for her, but that *she* wasn't at liberty to answer. The turnabout might've been amusing. Except it was anything but.

As was this rapidly deteriorating interview.

John jerked his chin toward the blond strands that had

escaped her makeshift bun. "You dyed your hair to play Rachel, didn't you?"

Oh, boy. There was only one place this was headed.

Still, she nodded.

What other option did she have? The chances of his forgiving her were already slim to none. If she lied to him now, there was no chance.

"So, you were in that bar, looking like you did, to meet *him*."

She managed another nod.

As did he. "But you got me. And since Evan had refused to bite, you were stuck with me—because he was in my house."

"Yes."

LaCroix, bastard that he was, was right. John would never forgive her. How could he? She wasn't sure she could get there herself.

"Just to clarify, if Evan had been interested, you'd have left with him that night instead of me."

"John—"

"Answer the question, *Chief*."

Chief. Not Regan, not Agent Chase. Hell, not even Rachel.

"Yes."

The fury had returned, and it was everywhere now. In that scorching stare and in that clipped jaw. In those rigid shoulders and those tightly bunched muscles. And in that telltale pulse. For the first time since they'd met, the latter's thunderous pace revealed more than she wanted to know. John was beyond livid. With her. "There's no article, then. But you have been writing up every moment you've spent with me, haven't you? Everything we've said. Everything we've *done*."

Not *everything*.

But would he believe her?

She opened her mouth to tell him, despite the recorder, only to snap it shut as the door to the interview room blew inward. A split second later, Jelly's jubilant, freckled grin barreled inside.

"Holy crap, Prez—you did it! The boss was right; you are the master of undercover. You can get to *anyone*. LaCroix's spilling as we speak, including how, where and why he built that bomb. He's—" The rest died in his throat, drowned by the flash flood of scarlet that rivaled the man's hair as Jelly finally realized who was seated across the table from her.

It was too late. The damage had been done.

John stood.

She didn't even rate a parting glance as he executed a stiff turn and strode to the door. John stopped beside her fellow agent, but didn't deign to look at Jelly either. "Am I finished?"

The scarlet tide bled all the way down to bloodless white as Jelly swallowed audibly—and risked a glance at her.

She nodded.

Another swallow as he shifted his attention back to John. "Yes, sir. We'll have your statement transcribed. We'll call when it's ready to be signed."

"Excellent. See that *you* do." The implication was as clear as it was humiliating. Worse, the dam that John had carefully wedged up against his anger since he'd discovered her true identity was about to blow.

John knew it too, because he didn't say another word. He left.

Regan stood and crossed the room.

"Fuck, Prez. I'm sorry—"

Unlike John, she did spare Jelly a glance as she paused at his side. "Not your fault." This was all on her, and she knew it. "Turn off the recorder and watch those two evidence bags for me, will you? I'll be back to log it all in."

"Sure thing."

She followed John out the door. She had to double-time down the hall and out of the building to catch up with him in the darkened parking lot. He was closing in on the cluster of sand-colored trucks and Humvees. His silver Wrangler appeared to be tucked in the middle. So much for situational awareness. If she hadn't been so unsettled by that showdown with LaCroix when she'd arrived back here, she might've seen the Wrangler then and realized John was waiting inside.

Though, really, would that have changed any of this?

Still, she had to try.

"Wait! Please, John, let me—" She broke off as he whirled about to confront her beside the bumper of the nearest Humvee.

"Explain? Oh, feel free, *Chief*. What exactly was going through your head when you came over to console me so very *sweetly* tonight?"

Shit. He really had survived the day from hell, hadn't he?

The vestiges were all right there in his face, threatening to break free. The stress of walking that classified line between an eager Ertonç and a recalcitrant Saniye, as the Pentagon—and quite possibly the White House—breathed down his neck with expectant breath. Dealing with LaCroix and their disintegrating friendship as he'd tried to support the man amid the sergeant's grief and burgeoning anger. His guilt over failing to help LaCroix, let alone discern what the sergeant was plotting in time to talk him down, much less thwart him from nearly killing Olan, Saniye and those kids. The risk to NATO. Not to mention losing yet another fellow soldier and good friend to that Iraqi bombing in the middle of it all.

And now her.

She reached out to touch his arm. It was a mistake.

The rage was all but radiating off him. He wasn't even trying to absorb it anymore as he jerked back. Glared down at her. "*Well?*"

"I wanted to tell you. I was going to."

"Really? And was that confession scheduled for before or

after that first time, up against the wall in my living room? Or how about the second, in my bed? Or the *third*? Or how about while you were waiting for me to fall asleep so you could crawl out of my arms and sneak into my kitchen to rifle though my garbage? Or maybe you just planned on waiting until the bitter end, gathering it all up and hoarding the juicy details of my goddamned stupidity before confessing all when you took the stand at Evan's court-martial?"

"That's not—"

He shook his head, cutting her off again. "The funny thing is, I knew something was wrong when I woke. Call me crazy, but I could feel it. Still, part of me hoped you got called out on a story and just...didn't have time to let me know. Not even with a pithy text. The other part of me—and you're going to love this— thought, hey, she's young. Tonight was intense. She just needs time to process. Hell, when I found Saniye's address in that laptop, I was relieved you'd left. I didn't want Evan anywhere near you 'til I'd figured things out, especially since our budding relationship just seemed to piss him off. What a goddamned crock. There is no relationship. There never was. Not for you. It was all lies—*all of it.*"

"It wasn't. John, I swear—"

The side of his fist slammed into the back of the Humvee, causing two-and-a-half tons of Army steel to rattle, along with her skull and her teeth. Her shock must've shown because he jerked his hand down, dragging the night air in deep as he worked to get that crackling temper back under control.

He finally purged his breath and nodded. "Fine. You want to explain, go ahead. Tell me, which one of your many heartfelt confessions was actually true? And do be honest, honey, because I'd really like to know. Your mom's death? Your bastard of a grandfather? The sob story about the foster homes?" He stepped closer, leaned down. "Was your father even a cop? *Was* he shot in the line of duty? Or was it all just some carefully crafted fairytale designed to reel me in once you got a good look at all the childhood *shit* in my BI?"

She opened her mouth, then closed it. As much as she wanted to explain, she couldn't. Not like this. Not here, in the middle of the parking lot.

Disgust darkened John's scowl as he straightened. "Yeah, I thought so. I gotta hand it to you. Your partner was right. You are *outstanding* at what you do. Mata Hari in the flesh. And even better in bed. And the lies? You're right up there with my old man. Hell, you surpassed him—and you punch a *lot* lower and a hell of a lot harder. So congratulations, Chief. First place to you. I hope the win was worth it."

It wasn't. Because he was wrong. She hadn't won.

She'd lost everything.

She'd lost him.

Who was she kidding? John had never been hers. Not really. Nor did he want to be. Because he'd already turned and walked away. Again. As much as she hated herself for it, she stood there and waited as John got into his Wrangler, started the engine, and pulled out of the lot. She needn't have bothered.

He never looked back.

9

T he phone rang as Regan added the final touch to her latest cover identity. A swift glance at the caller ID had her truly smiling for the first time in weeks. She hadn't spoken to Mira in almost a month. Not since the NCIS agent had returned to the States to resume plowing through her own, ever-increasing caseload.

Regan closed the file on her laptop and swapped it for the phone on her coffee table. There'd be time enough to absorb the finer details of Corporal ReAnne Shelby in the morning. "Hey, stranger. What's up?"

Mira's sigh filled the line. "I know, I know. I've been MIA again. I've been meaning to call. I've just had too much filth to wade through for a case."

"You want to talk about it?"

"I can't. Not yet, anyway. But thanks." She could hear Mira's TV on in the background. The talking heads were going at it over something, but she couldn't make out what the argument was about. "So, how have you been? Have you heard anything from King Kong?"

"Nope." And it stung. Still.

Since it had been a solid month since John had walked out on her in that parking lot, she wasn't likely to hear from him either.

And there was the rest.

"Jelly saw him when he came in to sign his statement. John left a couple weeks later." They wouldn't even have to track him down for the court-martial.

There wasn't going to be one.

Sergeant LaCroix had pled guilty to a host of charges and had been busted down to Private LaCroix. He'd even admitted that he and Scott Platt had reconnected after LaCroix had referred Carys Kaide to the disgraced Pentagon employee eighteen months earlier when Carys and her Syrian NGO had come up short on critical medical supplies. Platt had been happy to provide "diverted" US military stock...at a price. Within the week, LaCroix—also stripped of his Special Forces tab and Army medals—would be enjoying his new, scaled down, maximum-security accommodations located inside the US Disciplinary Barracks at Fort Leavenworth, Kansas.

She'd thought it odd that LaCroix had gone down without fighting, but then, LaCroix was odd. Especially now. She'd gone to see him a few days ago to wrap up her case file and inform him of his pending flight to the States. He'd spent the entire hour just staring at her, smirking.

As for John—

"Rae, are you saying Garrison left? As in, the captain's no longer in Germany?"

"Correct."

"When's he due to return?"

He wasn't. "According to Jelly, he received orders to Fort Bragg." John would be deploying to yet another hotspot from there soon enough.

Damn it—stop. He wasn't hers to worry about. He never had been.

Regan abandoned the couch and headed for the door to her tiny Vilseck apartment. Midnight had come and gone. It was time to lock up and crawl into bed for yet another sleepless night. She should probably bring her laptop. Might as well fire it back up and work on memorizing Shelby's backstory.

It beat counting her many screwups and sins in lieu of sheep.

"Oh, hon. I'm so sorry."

Yeah, so was she. But that didn't change anything, did it? Least of all, this malaise she couldn't seem to push through.

At least something good had come from the investigation. Saniye had met with the general the morning after they'd arrested LaCroix. Not only had father and daughter reconciled, but the entire Karmandi family had disappeared into thin air last week, along with Ertonç. It seemed new identities were in order. And this time, the general had been included—following a tragic collision with a fuel truck on the autobahn that managed to burn so hot, there was nothing left of the man but the DNA they'd managed to extract from a tooth.

She had no idea where they'd gone. Nor did she want to know.

It was better that way. Just as she was better off without John. Lord knew he was definitely better off without her.

Apprehension filtered through the malaise.

"Mira?" For someone who'd called to chat, the woman wasn't being all that chatty.

"Yeah?"

"What's wrong?" Washington, DC, was six hours behind Germany, something the NCIS agent was well aware of. "Why are you calling this late?" And why was she asking about John?

And there was that odd, reluctant tension on her friend's end of the line. Regan could feel it thickening in the silence. As though Mira had something significant to say...but couldn't quite bring herself to say it.

Nausea sloshed into her gut as she glanced across the room. Her TV was off. Mira's wasn't. And she was calling.

Had there been a training accident at Bragg? Or was John already deployed? Had something happened? Another one of those goddamned bombings in the world?

Was he injured—or worse?

The nausea began to churn in earnest. "Is John...okay?"

"He's fine—at least, I think so. I haven't spoken to him since I left Hohenfels. But, uh, turn on the news."

Regan was already striding toward the TV. If Mira wasn't calling about John, had someone figured out Ertonç wasn't really dead—and had taken pains to ensure the man became so?

Too tense to translate, Regan snatched the remote off the coffee table and punched in the channel number for the local, English-language cable news network.

She needn't have bothered. The succession of photos that were flashing across the screen transcended language.

"*Sweet Jesus.*"

Whoever said a picture was worth a thousand words had woefully underestimated the amount. Because those were worth a million. At least to her. The photos were of Sergeant First Class LaCroix, John Garrison...and her. But while John's face had been thoughtfully blurred out by the network, LaCroix's and hers had not. She rated several pictures, in fact. Her official Army mugshot, a candid of her in civilian clothes...and a slightly out-of-focus view of her with Rachel Pace's hair before she'd had a chance to have it dyed back to her normal, muddy brown.

The commentary? That was *so* much worse.

The remote clattered to the floor.

Her phone nearly followed.

"Yeah, I know, Rae. It's bad." She could hear Mira grinding her teeth. "The upshot? According to LaCroix's lawyer, the Army knowingly pimped you out. Basically, they're saying you set out to screw Garrison in order to make your case. Don't worry. It won't hold up, and you know it. So does LaCroix. He's just pissed. Even his bastard of a lawyer admitted John wasn't the target of the investigation. Heck, you'd cleared him of suspicion several times over before that night—along with me *and* Agent Jelling."

She nodded numbly. She had. They all had.

But that wouldn't matter, would it?

Not to her still gun-shy boss and certainly not to John. In fact, John's anger and humiliation were bound to be reinforced by this. Magnified.

LaCroix had planned on that too. The bastard's twisted, personal payback for John bringing that laptop of his into CID and signing a statement regarding the breach of those encrypted files on John's work computer.

She finally understood that smirk.

LaCroix had gotten his revenge after all, and then some. General Ertonç was alive, but his career was toast. Saniye, her husband and their kids had been uprooted and forced into hiding. Hell, even Turkey was eyeing NATO though a serious squint—as they fluttered their geo-political lashes and blew kisses at Russia.

And as for her? She'd dared to thwart LaCroix's initial plans by intercepting that first, physical, bomb—so the sergeant had ruthlessly constructed another. This second one might have been virtual and crafted on the fly, but with it, LaCroix had succeeded in blowing her career as an active, undercover investigative asset into oblivion.

She could still feel the molten shrapnel raining down. The

devil with the slur against her reputation, her *face* was on the international news.

What the hell was she supposed to do now?

∼

Thanks so much for reading the introductory prequel to my Deception Point military detective series. I hope you enjoyed it! As you know, an author's career is built on reviews. Please take a moment to leave a quick comment or an in-depth review for your fellow readers

HERE.

∼

Are you ready for Regan's 1st,
full-blown murder case?

CLICK HERE *to get your copy of* **Blind Edge**, *Book 2 in the Deception Point Military Detective Thriller Series. Or turn the page for a sneak peek!*

WHAT'S NEXT?

What if the one person you can't trust...is yourself?

US Army Detective Regan Chase spent years lying for her country.

Until she was caught.

Her reputation as the military's premier undercover chameleon in tatters, Regan's been shunted to a Stateside post and reassigned to the grunt work of Army CID—investigations. First up, the brutal stabbing of a soldier's wife.

Instead of the domestic homicide she expects, Regan confronts the first in a series of murders and suicides brought on by the violent hallucinations plaguing a twelve-man Special Forces A-Team just back from Afghanistan. A team led by Regan's ex-lover. The very soldier responsible for the decimation of her undercover career.

As the murders and suicides mount, Regan clashes with an unforgiving, uncooperative and dangerously secretive John Garrison—and an even more secretive US Army.

The Army knows she and John have history. So why hasn't she been reassigned?

Someone wants Regan on the case. But they also want her

off her game. They're depending on it. Why else is she being followed?

What happened in that Afghan cave? Why is the Army willing to risk an entire Special Forces team to keep it secret?

Regan won't stop until she finds out. But by then, it may be too late. Another name may have already been added to that growing list of victims.

Her own.

Blind Edge is now available.

CLICK HERE to grab your copy of Blind Edge & keep reading this gripping series today!
Or turn the page for a sneak peak.

SNEAK PEEK - BLIND EDGE

BOOK 2 IN THE DECEPTION POINT MILITARY THRILLER SERIES

Prologue

THE BIBLE WAS WRONG. Vengeance didn't belong to the Lord. It belonged to him.

To them.

To the twelve soldiers who'd stumbled out of that dank, icy cave, each as consumed as he was by the malevolence that had been carved into their souls. A second later, the night breeze shifted—and he caught a whiff of *him*. He couldn't be sure if that rotting piece of camel dung had been left behind as a lookout or if the bastard was part of a squad waiting to ambush his team. When the combined experiences of countless covert missions locked in, allowing him to place the stench wafting down along with stale sweat and pure evil, he no longer cared. Because once again, he smelled blood.

Fresh blood.

It permeated the air outside the cave, as did the need for retribution. As his fellow soldiers faded into the wind-sheared boulders, he knew they felt it too.

By God, they would all taste it.

Soon.

He shot out on point. There was no need to glance behind as he reached the base of the cliff and shouldered his rifle. His team had followed, protecting his back as they'd done every op these past months. The trust freed him to focus on their unspoken mission. On the blood pooling around seven bodies laid out on the floor of that cavern, and then some. He tucked the blade of his knife between his teeth and began to climb. Rock tore at his fingers as he jammed them into crevice after crevice, causing his own blood to mingle with the death still staining his hands. Moments later, he stopped, locking the toes of his boots to a narrow ledge as he scanned the dark.

Nothing.

He resumed his climb. The same moonless night that cloaked his prey protected him and his team. As long as they were mute, they were safe. Unless—

Shit!

He froze as the wind shifted, shooting his own stench heavenward. He caught the answering scuffle of panicked boots.

Too late, bastard.

He was almost there.

His position compromised, he grabbed a scrub pine, using it to whiplash up the remaining three feet of cliff.

Loose rock bit into his soles, causing him to skid to a halt two yards from his prey. The wind shifted once more, whipping a filthy turban from the bastard's face. A second later, he was staring into pure, bearded hatred as an AK47 rifle swung up. He grabbed his knife and lunged forward. Blood gushed over his knuckles as he buried the blade to its hilt. He hauled the bastard in closer, staring deep into that blackened gaze, for the first time in his life embracing the carnal satisfaction that seared in on a close-quarters kill—until suddenly, inexplicably, the gaze wavered...then slowly disintegrated altogether.

To his horror, it coalesced once more, this time into a soft blue hue he knew all too well.

Sweet Jesus—*no!*

It was a lie. A trick. An illusion. This latest flood of adrenaline had simply been too much to absorb. That was all.

Goddamn it, that was *all.*

He'd never know how he managed to hold his heart together as he released the knife and brought his fingers to his eyes. He rubbed them over and over, praying harder than he'd ever prayed as he sank to his knees. But as he blinked through his tears and forced himself to focus on the river of scarlet gushing into the snow, he knew it was true. The body in his arms wasn't that of his enemy. Nor was he in some freezing mountain pass half a world away. He was in his own backyard.

And he'd just murdered the woman he loved.

≈

Now I lay me down to sleep,
 I pray the Lord my soul to keep.

If I should kill before I wake,
 I pray the Lord it's my enemy I take.

≈

Chapter 1

Military Police Station
 Fort Campbell, Kentucky

US ARMY SPECIAL AGENT Regan Chase stared at the five-foot fir anchoring the corner of the deserted lounge. A rainbow of ornaments dangled from the tree's artificial limbs along with hundreds of twinkling lights, each doing its damnedest to infect her with an equally artificial promise of home, hearth and simpering happiness. Fifteen months ago, she might've succumbed. Tonight, that phony fir simply underscored the three tenets of truth Regan had crashed into at the tender age of six. One, no one sat around the North Pole stuffing sacks with free toys. Two, reindeer couldn't fly. And three, if there ever had been some jolly old geezer looking out for the boys and girls of the world, he'd been fired for incompetence a long time ago.

The current proof was handcuffed to a stall in the military police station's latrine, attempting to purge what appeared to be an entire fifth of nauseatingly ripe booze. Unfortunately, the majority of the alcohol had long since made it into the man's bloodstream. Even more unfortunate, Regan had no idea whose bloodstream said booze was currently coursing through.

Not only had their drunken John Doe been arrested sans driver's license and military ID, he'd stolen the pickup he'd used in tonight's carnage.

Regan turned her back on the tree and headed for the coffee table at the rear of the lounge, sighing as she sank into one of the vinyl chairs. She reached past a bowl of cellophane-wrapped candy canes to snag the stack of photos she'd queued into the duty sergeant's printer upon her arrival. The close-up of the stolen pickup's silver grill splattered with blood flaunted its own obscene contribution to the night's festivities. The scarlet slush adhering to the tires beneath provided even more proof of yet another Christmas shot to hell.

Make that crushed.

Regan studied the remaining dozen photos. From the angle and depth of the furrows running the length of the snowy street,

John Doe hadn't tried to slow down, much less swerve. Instead, he'd plowed into a trio of teenagers making the rounds of Fort Campbell's senior officer housing and belting out carols to the commanding general himself. One of the boys had suffered a broken leg. Another had dislocated his shoulder as he'd tried to wrench his younger brother out of the way of the truck's relentless headlights. Unfortunately, he'd failed.

As far as Regan knew, the kid was still in surgery.

She should phone the hospital. Find out if he'd made it to recovery. She was about to retrieve her cellphone when the door opened. A lanky, red-haired specialist strode in, a ring-sized, gift-wrapped box in his left hand, the naked fingers of a curvaceous blond in his right.

The specialist paused as he spotted Regan. Flushed. "Sorry, Chief. Thought the lounge was vacant."

He held his breath as he waited. Regan knew why. She'd transferred to Fort Campbell's Criminal Investigation Division two weeks earlier. Not quite long enough for the resident military policemen to know if CID's newest investigator had a poker up her ass regarding midnight rendezvous while on duty, even on holidays.

Regan scooped the photos off the table, tucking them into the oversized cargo pocket on the thigh of her camouflaged Army Combat Uniform as she stood. She scanned the name tag on the soldier's matching ACUs as she grabbed her parka and patrol cap. "It's all yours, Specialist Jasik. I was about to leave for the hospital."

Why not?

She wouldn't be getting a decent statement until their drunken Doe sobered up. Given the stunning 0.32 the man had blown on their breathalyzer, that would be a good eight hours, at least. If the man didn't plunge into a coma first.

Jasik relaxed. He led the blond to the couch as Regan passed.

"Thanks, Chief. And Merry Christmas."

Regan peeled back the velcroed grosgrain covering of her combat watch and glanced at the digital readout: 0003. So it was —all three minutes of it. Though what was so merry about it, she had no idea. But that was her problem. Or so she'd been told.

Regan returned the salutation anyway, donning her camouflaged parka and cap as she departed the lounge. Nodding to the duty sergeant, she pushed the glass doors open. Icy wind whipped across a freshly salted walk, kicking up snowflakes from the two-foot banks scraped to the sides. The flakes stung her eyes and chapped her cheeks as she passed a pair of recently de-iced police cruisers at the head of the dimly lit lot.

By the time Regan reached her Explorer, she was looking forward to the impromptu hospital visit. It would give her a chance to stop by the ER and commiserate with Gil. Like her, he had a habit of volunteering for Christmas duty.

For an entirely different reason, though.

Regan unlocked her SUV. Exhaust plumed as she started the engine. Grabbing her ice scraper from the door, she cleared the latest layer of snow from her front windshield. She was finishing the rear when an ear-splitting wail rent the air.

Ambulance. On post.

Judging from its Doppler, it was headed away from the hospital.

The police station's door whipped open, confirming her hunch. A trio of ACU-clad military policemen vaulted into the night, their combat boots thundering down the salted walk. The first two MPs peeled off and piled into the closest de-iced cruiser. The third headed straight for her.

Regan recognized the soldier's tall, ebony frame: Staff Sergeant Otis T. Wickham.

They'd met in front of their drunken Doe's blood-splattered pickup, where they'd also reached the conclusion that Doe's intended target did indeed appear to be the trio of caroling kids and not the commanding general. One look at the tension locking the MP's jaw as he reached her side told her that whatever had gone down was bad.

He popped a salute. "Evenin', Chief. There's been a stabbing in Stryker Housing. Victim's a woman. The captain wants you there. No specifics, but it's gotta be bad. The husband called it in. Man's Special Forces—and he was downright frantic."

Regan tossed the ice scraper inside the Explorer. "Get in."

Wickham wedged his bulk into her passenger seat as she hit the emergency lights and peeled out after the shrieking cruiser. They fishtailed onto Forest Road, neither of them speaking. It was for the best. Four-wheel drive or not, it took all her concentration to keep up with the cruiser as they reached the entrance to Fort Campbell's snowbound Stryker Family Housing. The strobes of the now-silent ambulance bathed the neighborhood in an eerily festive red, ushering them to a cookie-cutter brick-and-vinyl duplex at the end of the street.

Regan brought the SUV to a halt within kissing distance of the cruiser and killed her siren.

Doors slammed as she and the MPs bailed out.

She recognized the closest as the gift-bearing soldier from the lounge. Specialist Jasik had traded the curvaceous blond for a black, thirty-something private. Staff Sergeant Wickham motioned Jasik to his side. The private headed for the end of the drive to round up the pajama-clad rubberneckers. Life-saving gear in hand, a trio of paramedics waited impatiently for the official all-clear from the MPs.

Regan withdrew her 9mm Sig Sauer from its holster at her outer right thigh as Wickham and Jasik retrieved their M9s before killing the volume on their police radios. Save for the crush of snow, silence reigned as they approached the duplex. A life-sized Santa cutout decorated the front door. A cursory glance at the knob revealed no obvious sign of forced entry. The brass plate above the mail slot provided a name and a rank: Sergeant Patrick Blessing.

Regan moved to the right of Santa's corpulent belly as Wickham assumed the left. Jasik was moving into position when the door opened.

Three 9mms whipped up, zeroed in.

A woman froze in the entryway. Roughly five feet tall, Hispanic, mid-twenties. She was dressed in a long-sleeved pink flannel nightgown and fleece-lined moccasins. Given her wide eyes and rigid spine, she was more startled than they. But she wasn't Mrs. Blessing. Though her cuffs were splattered with blood, the woman appeared uninjured. Definitely not stabbed.

She swallowed firmly. "She—uh—Danielle's out back. I live next door. My husband's a medic." Her voice dropped to a whisper. "He's with them now."

Regan lowered her Sig. The MPs followed suit as the woman waved them in.

Regan tipped her head toward Wickham. She might be senior in rank, but right now, she was junior to the staff sergeant's on-post experience. That included knowledge of Stryker's floor plans. Protocol dictated they assume the suspect was on the premises, possibly controlling the actions of the medic's wife—and search accordingly.

Wickham clipped a nod as he and Jasik headed down the hall.

Regan caught the neighbor's gaze. "Stay here."

The relief swirling into her tear-stained face assured Regan she would. The woman had already seen more than she wanted, and it had shaken her to her core. As Regan passed through the kitchen to join Wickham and Jasik at the sliding glass door in the dining room, she realized why the neighbor was so rattled.

They all did.

They'd found Mrs. Blessing. She was twenty feet away, lying in the snow on her back, clad in a sleeveless, floral nightgown bunched beneath her breasts. Like her neighbor, Danielle was delicate, dark-haired and—despite the gray cast to her flesh—almost painfully pretty. But there was nothing pretty about the knife embedded in her belly. Two men knelt along the woman's left. Judging from his sobs, Regan assumed the bare-chested man just past the woman's head, smoothing curls, was her husband. That pegged the man at her torso, leaning over to blow air through her lips, as the medic. Like the husband, the medic had removed his T-shirt. The shirts were packed around the hilt of the knife, immobilizing the blade in a desperate attempt to keep the flow of blood corked. Given the amount of red saturating the cotton, it wasn't working. Danielle Blessing was bleeding out. But that wasn't the worst of it.

She was pregnant.

"Jesus H. Chri—" Jasik swallowed the rest.

The MP regained his composure and grabbed his radio to yell for the paramedics as Regan and Wickham shot through the open slider and across the snow. She'd have to trust that Jasik knew enough to secure the interior of the duplex after his call.

Regan dropped to her knees opposite the medic as the man thumped out a series of chest compressions. Staff Sergeant Wickham was two seconds behind and two inches beside her.

Odds were, they were already too late.

Danielle Blessing's abdomen was extremely distended—

even for a third trimester—and rock hard. An oddly sweet odor wafted up from the makeshift packing, mixing with the cloying stench of blood. It was a scent Regan would recognize anywhere: amniotic fluid. Worse, scarlet seeped from between the woman's thighs, pooling amid the snow.

Regan holstered her Sig and ripped off her camouflaged parka. "What have you got?"

The medic looked up. "No breathing, no pulse. Been that way since I got here—six damned minutes ago." The rest was in his eyes. *Hopeless.*

The medic continued thumping regardless. Working around the knife, she and Wickham covered the woman's lower abdomen, thighs and calves with their coats. Danielle's feet were still exposed to the snow and midnight air. Like her face, they were beyond gray.

Regan shook her head as the medic completed his latest round of chest compressions. "I've got it." She sealed her mouth to the woman's lips. They were ice-cold and unresponsive.

Wickham took over the compressions as Regan finished her breaths. But for the husband's raw sobs and Wickham's thumping, silence filled the night.

Two more rounds of breath, and Regan lost her job. So did Wickham. The paramedics had arrived.

Blessing's neighbor dragged the sergeant to his feet as she and Wickham scrambled out of the way. Two of the paramedics dropped their gear and knelt to double-check Danielle's airway and non-existent vitals as a third probed the saturated T-shirts. Ceding to the inevitable, Regan turned toward the duplex. Jasik stood at the kitchen window, his initial search evidently complete.

The MP shook his head. If someone had broken into the Blessings' home, he or she was gone now.

The slider was still open. The medic had reached the snow-covered steps and stood to the left. Sergeant Blessing had turned and slumped down at the top, halfway inside the slider's frame, his naked feet buried in a drift, his dark head bowing over bloodstained hands, and he was shaking.

From grief? Or guilt?

Unfortunately, she knew. As with the icy furrows left by a drunken Doe's stolen pickup, the snow provided the proof.

Footprints.

They covered the yard. But upon their arrival, there'd been but four telling sets. Once Regan eliminated those left by the his-and-her moccasins of the medic and his wife, she was left with a single, composite trail of overlapping, bare footprints. The leading prints were woefully petite; the following, unusually large. Both sets were dug into the snow as if their owners had torn down the slider's steps and across the yard...all the way to where Danielle lay. Finally, there was the blood. Save for the scarlet slush surrounding the body, there was no sign of splatter—at the slider or along the trail.

For some reason, Sergeant Blessing had deliberately chased and *then* stabbed his wife.

Regan turned to Wickham. "I'll take the husband, question him inside. You take the neighbor. Stay out here." She glanced at the paramedics. "They might need to talk to him." Though she doubted it. There was nothing the sergeant could say that would help his wife now.

Danielle Blessing had been placed on a spine board, stripped down to gray, oozing flesh and redressed with several trauma pads. Half a dozen rolls of Kling gauze anchored the pads and the hilt of the knife. As the brawnier of the paramedics finished intubating the woman's throat and began manually pumping oxygen into her lungs via a big valve mask, his female partner attached the leads of a portable electrocardiogram to Danielle's shoulders and left hip.

Silence had long since given way to a calm, steady stream of medical jargon.

"Patient on cardiac monitor."

"IV spiked on blood set. One thousand milliliters NS. Starting second line—LR on a Macro drip, sixteen gauge."

"I still can't get a pulse."

Judging from that last—not to mention the wad of fresh dressing one of the paramedics used to dry off Danielle's chest —the next step involved shocks. In a perfect world, the woman's heart would restart. But the world was far from perfect. Regan had learned that the hard way. Given that this woman's heart had already been subjected to eight-plus minutes of unsuccessful CPR, the odds that she'd recover were all but nonexistent.

Regan shifted her attention to Wickham. "Ready, Staff Sergeant?"

His nod was stoic. But his sigh was resigned. Bitter. "Merry Christmas."

The past crowded in despite Regan's attempts to keep it at bay. She shook it off. "Yeah."

Wickham doffed his camouflaged cap as they headed for the slider. Though his bald scalp was exposed to the winter air, he appeared not to notice. She couldn't seem to feel the cold either. Nor did the medic.

The husband was still staring at his hands, shaking.

Regan exchanged a knowing frown with Wickham as she reached for her handcuffs. Two strides later, the distinctive whine of a cardiac defibrillator charging filled the night.

And then, "*Clear!*"

A dull thud followed.

The shocks had begun. Even if Danielle made it, there was no hope for her baby. If that knife hadn't killed it, the electrical jolts would. Judging by the panic on the husband's face as he shot to his feet, Sergeant Blessing had figured it out.

"Wait!"

The neighbor grabbed Blessing's right arm. Jasik leapt through the open side of the slider and pinned Blessing's left.

"Charging to three hundred."

Blessing thrashed, nearly knocking both his captors to the ground. "Goddamn it! The *baby*—"

"Clear!"

Jasik regained his hold and drove Blessing to his knees, sealing the sergeant's shins to the ground as the paramedics ripped through the final steps of ECG protocol. As they hit three hundred sixty joules—for the third agonizing time—Blessing accepted the inescapable. His wife and child were dead.

He slumped into the snow as Jasik and the neighbor loosened their grips. A soft keening filled the night, laying waste to every one of Regan's meticulously honed defenses.

Her eyes burned. Her heart followed.

She pulled herself together and tossed her handcuffs to Jasik, her unspoken order clear. *Get it over with.*

Jasik caught the cuffs neatly and bent down.

That was as far as he got.

One moment the lanky MP was behind Sergeant Blessing, pushing him to his knees; the next, Blessing had twisted about, bashing his forehead into Jasik's skull.

A sharp grunt filled the air.

Regan caught the flash of blackened metal as Blessing ripped the 9mm from Jasik's holster. She lunged across the remaining three feet of snow, launching herself at Blessing as the weapon's barrel swung up.

She was too late.

The 9mm's retort reverberated through Regan as she and Blessing smashed into the slider.

CLICK HERE *to get your copy of Blind Edge & keep reading this gripping series!*

Make sure you're on Candace's list, so you know all about her new releases, special giveaways and Reader Crew extras.

You can do that here: candaceirving.com/newsletter

The best part of writing is connecting with readers. Occasionally, I send out newsletters with details on upcoming releases, current free books & special subscriber giveaways.

To snag your Reader Crew Extras, sign up here:
www.CandaceIrving.com

MEET THE AUTHOR

CANDACE IRVING is the daughter of a librarian and a retired US Navy chief. Candace grew up in the Philippines, Germany, and all over the United States. Her senior year of high school, she enlisted in the US Army. Following basic training, she transferred to the Navy's ROTC program at the University of Texas-Austin. While at UT, she spent a summer in Washington, DC, as a Congressional Intern. She also worked security for the UT Police.

BA in Political Science in hand, Candace was commissioned as an ensign in the US Navy and sent to Surface Warfare Officer's School to learn to drive warships. From there, she followed her father to sea.

Candace is married to her favorite soldier, a former US Army Combat Engineer. They live in the American Midwest, where the Army/Navy football game is avidly watched and argued over every year.

Go Navy; Beat Army!

Candace also writes military romantic suspense under the name Candace Irvin—without the "g"!

Email Candace at www.CandaceIrving.com
or connect via:

ALSO BY CANDACE IRVING

Deception Point Military Detective Thrillers:

AIMPOINT

Has an elite explosives expert turned terrorist? Army Detective Regan Chase is ordered to use her budding relationship with his housemate —John Garrison—to find out. But John is hiding something too. Has the war-weary Special Forces captain been turned as well? As Regan's investigation deepens, lines are crossed—personal and professional. Even if Regan succeeds in thwarting a horrific bombing on German soil, what will the fallout do to her career?

A DECEPTION POINT MILITARY DETECTIVE THRILLER: A REGAN CHASE NOVELLA & BOOK 1 IN THE SERIES

BLIND EDGE

Army Detective Regan Chase responds to a series of murders and suicides brought on by the violent hallucinations plaguing a Special Forces A-Team—a team led by Regan's ex, John Garrison. Regan quickly clashes with an unforgiving, uncooperative and dangerously secretive John—and an even more secretive US Army. What really happened during that Afghan cave mission? As Regan pushes for answers, the murders and suicides continue to mount. By the time the Army comes clean, it may be too late. Regan's death warrant has already been signed—by John's hands.

A DECEPTION POINT MILITARY DETECTIVE THRILLER: BOOK 2

BACKBLAST

Army Detective Regan Chase just solved the most horrific case of her career. The terrorist responsible refuses to speak to anyone but her. The claim? There's a traitor in the Army. With the stakes critical, Regan heads for the government's newest classified interrogation site: A US Navy warship at sea. There, Regan uncovers a second, deadlier, terror plot that leads all the way to a US embassy—and beyond. Once again, Regan's on the verge of losing her life—and another far more valuable to her than her own...

A DECEPTION POINT MILITARY DETECTIVE THRILLER: BOOK 3

CHOKEPOINT

When a US Navy captain is brutally murdered, NCIS Special Agent Mira Ellis investigates. As Mira follows the killer to a ship hijacked at sea, the ties to her own past multiply. Mira doesn't know who to trust—including her partner. A decorated, former Navy SEAL of Saudi descent, Sam Riyad lied to an Army investigator during a terror case and undermined the mission of a Special Forces major. Whose side is Riyad really on? The fate of the Navy—and the world—depends on the answer.

A DECEPTION POINT MILITARY DETECTIVE THRILLER: BOOK 4

~MORE DECEPTION POINT DETECTIVE THRILLERS COMING SOON~

Hidden Valor Military Veteran Suspense:

THE GARBAGE MAN

Former Army detective Kate Holland spent years hiding from the world—and herself. Now a small-town cop, the past catches up when a fellow vet is left along a backroad...in pieces. Years earlier, Kate spent eleven hours as a POW. Her Silver Star write-up says she killed eleven terrorists to avoid staying longer. But Kate has no memory of the deaths. And now, bizarre clues are cropping up. Is Kate finally losing her grip on reality? As the murders multiply, Kate must confront her demons...even as she finds herself in the killer's crosshairs.

A Hidden Valor Military Veteran Suspense: Book 1

IN THE NAME OF

Kate Holland finally remembers her eleven hours as a POW in Afghanistan. She wishes she didn't. PTSD raging, Kate's ready to turn in her badge with the Braxton PD. But the wife of a Muslim US Army soldier was stabbed and left to burn in a field, and Kate's boss has turned to her. Kate suspects an honor killing...until another soldier's wife is found in the next town, also stabbed and burned. When a third wife is murdered, Kate uncovers a connection to a local doctor. But the doc is not all she appears to be. Worse, Kate's nightmares and her case have begun to clash. The fallout is deadly as Kate's lured back to where it all began.

A Hidden Valor Military Veteran Suspense: Book 2

BENEATH THE BONES

When skeletal remains are unearthed on a sandbar amid the Arkansas River, Deputy Kate Holland's world is rocked again. The bones belong to a soldier once stationed at a nearby National Guard post. The more Kate digs into the murdered soldier's life, the more connections she discovers between the victim, an old family friend...and her own father. Fresh bodies are turning up too. Will the clues her father missed all those years ago lead to the deaths of every officer on the Braxton police force—including Kate's?

A Hidden Valor Military Veteran Suspense: Book 3

~More Hidden Valor Books Coming Soon~

COPYRIGHT

eBook ISBN: 978-1-952413-06-3

Paperback ISBN: 978-1-952413-19-3

Large Print ISBN: 978-1-952413-22-3

Hardcover ISBN: 978-1-952413-33-9

AIMPOINT